RONA JAFFE

by *Rona Jaffe*

March '65

Dear Jean –
....Even though _you_ did it, the title
is still true for 170,000000, so there.
Love, love,
Rona.

Mr. Right Is Dead

A short novel and five stories

Simon and Schuster ❧ New York

Library of Congress Catalog Card Number: 65-15024
MANUFACTURED IN THE UNITED STATES OF AMERICA
By The Book Press, Brattleboro, Vermont
Designed by Helen Barrow

for P. S. L.

Contents

Mr. Right Is Dead

EVENTUALLY, people are willing to admit most of their flaws—greed, jealousy, pride, hostility—but the feeling they're most ashamed to admit is loneliness. I guess that's because it's the one weakness we all secretly feel should be the easiest to overcome, and we secretly feel guilty that we can't. Go out and *live*—right? Everyone fights loneliness his own way, but some people have to let others do it for them. And that reminds me of my friend Melba Toast, the skinniest stripper in America, who once jumped out of a dietetic cake at a Shriners' Club dinner. Melba is the greatest analgesic for pain since aspirin, but if you told her so she would glare at you for a moment, trying to decide if you meant it as a compliment or something dirty.

"What's analgesic?" she would say. "You're the one who reads a lot." But on the other hand, Mel reads Zen and seems to understand it better than I ever could.

She isn't a working stripper, and sometimes I suspect she never has been except for that dietetic cake. But she had to be something, because everyone is Something. An actress sounded too definite (credits, please), a model too indefinite (subject to the tabloid misinterpretation), she was too old to be a student and too young to be a mother-going-back-to-college, and so she became a stripper. Anyone can become anything he wants, even a doctor; all you have to do is buy a white coat, rent an office, and accept patients until you get caught. Melba Toast is that kind of stripper, except she wants to get caught faking. If she didn't get caught faking, how could she buy all those nice clothes and pay the rent on her $250-a-month apartment?

She's not a hooker, she's more of a cab-fare girl. "I'll get home fine, just give me a hundred dollars." She gets fifty dollars Ladies' Room money to tip an attendant who hasn't been there for years. Her clothes and fur coats are always being impounded for nonpayment of rent, or, as she puts it: "My land-lord was nice enough to put everything in storage for me until I come back." She takes quick flights of fancy and quick flights across the country in quest of someone she had two dates with a month before. She is impetuous and overactive and too insistent, but I like her and I'm always glad to see her, even when she's disappeared for six months without saying good-bye. Melba can take an enormous amount of abuse; I mean, you never have to return her phone calls or write to her or anything, and she always says hello as if she saw you yesterday. You never have to feel guilty with Melba, except when you won't lend her your evening gown.

Ordinarily I would never try to figure out why I like someone, except that most of Melba's friends do just that—sit around and try to figure out why they like her so much. They list their grievances (the afternoon phone call from a restaurant and the lunch check she stuck them with when they arrived, the way she name-drops celebrities she doesn't know in order to impress the taxi driver, the night she smoked pot in a taxi, etc.), and they list society's grievances (which are obvious), and they still admit Mel always makes them laugh when they're depressed, and feeds them when they're poor, and does turn up with those celebrities to introduce them to when they need a job.

Because I'm in analysis I try to dig deeper into my own motives, which is usually a bore, except that one of the reasons I like Melba, I have discovered, is that I am jealous of her. When I tell them that, my friends really wring their hands, and they tell me how she has no Real Friends and she's unhappy, and how I have Real Friends and I'm happy, and that I should discuss it with the doctor. But how many love affairs end with the man talking bitterly about the girl, claiming he dropped her, or saying she was a neurosis of the past and he's relieved she left? Compliments are given with clenched teeth after an affair has ended. But Melba's men, even years later, speak of her as if she's a special, kooky, marvelous person. I guess half of it is they can't admit they've been taken. And yet, secret motives aside, she moves in a glow of love, an afterglow, an afterglow of afterlove. And these men aren't all freaks or horrors: all of them are respectable, all of them are successful, most of them are famous, and some of them are even worth knowing. Mel has more unlisted phone numbers, I'd bet, than the phone company; she carries them with her at all times, and no one has ever been known to hang up on her.

It is true that someone can be rotten to you while you're there and then speak lovingly of you when you're safely not there, and so I'm sure many of us have present admirers who we *know* once hated us. It's easier to be tolerant of the past than the present; we change, we want to believe it was all lovely, for to remember it as it was would make us sad again. But I do think Mel is special, because she has a capacity for survival on her own terms that surpasses any I have ever seen. This is one of the things her friends think is tragic and her lovers have to admire.

It's one thing to survive on other people's terms; we all do that every day, and we call it adjustment, understanding, compromise, and some dead people even call it strength. But Melba not only gets along in life on her own terms, they are terms she has enthusiastically adopted from the silliest movie magazines, gossip columns, adolescent fantasies, and bits and pieces of the philosophies of one or two former boyfriends who happened to impress her. She has latched on to these clichés with a deadly earnestness that has made them come to life. When she lolls in the back seat of a chauffeur-driven "limo," or when she sits behind the wheel of a convertible—a really brand-new, ostentatious, too-horse-powered, mile-long, glistening, expensive, Grade-B-Movie-Star car —it means something to her that most of us cannot understand. And when she goes into the latest tourist trap, proud and serene on the arm of some insecure, married, middle-aged man with a health-club tan and a diamond ring on his pinkie, a tourist trap in which Diamond Ring (at Melba's instructions) whisks out a fifty-dollar bill and is then allowed to proceed to a tiny table, it means something to Melba that most of us cannot understand. She sits there in that noisy room, she listens to the music but does not dance, she gazes at all the pinking shears salesmen in their dinner jackets and the dress models in their vacant stares, she orders enormous quantities of food without looking at the menu and then does not eat a bite, she orders champagne—insisting the bottle be brought to the table before being poured so she can inspect the label—and then has only two sips; and she is happy.

Diamond Ring puts his hand on her knee. Melba opens her evening purse and takes out a handful of business cards.

"Do you know him? How about *him*? Oh, this one, I forget who he was. I got all these at one party last week. Do you have your card with you? Mmm, very nice."

She puts his card with the others. He notices small letters she has penciled on the margin of each card. He asks what they mean.

"*Real*—that means he's in real estate. *O*. means oil. *W.S*. stands for wealthy and a swinger. Now, what shall I write for you . . . ?"

She writes two letters on the corner of his card and smiles, then she puts all the cards back into her purse. She won't tell him what his letters mean. He wonders . . . he feels now he has been judged for some unaccountable crime . . . he hates her for it . . . and secretly, ashamedly, he wants her to like him, to change his letters to *G.L.*—Great Lover. For him, that is all he will know of love. He will appear again through the months, perhaps through the years. Melba never forgets anyone. Not the one with the yacht, nor the one with a private island, nor the one who sent her twelve dresses from Paris, nor the one with no money at all, for whom she cooked dinner every night for a week.

Perhaps I should start from the beginning, when I met her. It was the usual hot summer in New York. August in New York is a month of such total, perfect vileness that most New Yorkers pretend it doesn't exist. Unemployed actors lie sweating on second-hand beds in railroad apartments, looking at their fire escapes and the fire escapes of the people across the street. The ones with initiative flee to California to do television, and find hundreds of others with the same idea—and the same face. Employed actors are away doing movies or pilot films, or touring in stock, or on Broadway with air conditioning. It's different for girls. Girls seem to get along: they covey together like quail, they visit Mama for the summer, they find some fellow with air conditioning, or they get taken out a lot. There's always somebody with a back yard or a terrace, another girl, maybe, who's struck it lucky and wants company while the owner of the terrace is at the office. He is lucky that he is at the office, because offices are air conditioned, while terraces in New York are open-air sweatboxes assailed by a confetti of soot. Terraces are the chic equivalent of fire escapes except that fire escapes are useful.

All the losers are home in August; the winners are away. At night the losers come out of their lonely rooms and infest the bars. They drink beer, soak in the air conditioning, and exude hostility. Their faces never seem to lose that patina of perspiration they acquired all day in their rooms reading Casting Calls. They never walk in the park in the afternoons because it reminds them too much of their first year in New York when they did that all the time because it reminded them of home.

Since it is such an outside-of-the-home month, August is the best time to meet new men and have a romance. But August is the worst time to get involved with someone, because that's the month all the analysts are away. Yours *and* theirs. By the time the analysts get back the entire romance has flowered and been destroyed, and then it takes you at least until Christmas to get the guilt sorted out with the doctor: fifty-five percent *his,* forty-five percent *mine?*

Anyway, that summer I was taking ballet because I was trying to be an actress. You may have seen me on TV. I'm the young housewife who says, "Yes, it is a cleaner wash!" on the commercials; and also I'm the one who gets sick when the boss is coming for dinner; and once I was the one with the stringy, drab hair. It's pretty dispiriting to be the one with the yut husband and the jam-faced kids when my real life is bad enough, but I'm a good type because I look like anybody, and you can't knock the residuals. It's not a sure shot to stardom but I never do expect to play Juliet—maybe the Nurse when I get old enough, provided she has arthritis or migraine or menopause.

Anyway, the main reason I was taking ballet, aside from my natural urge for self-improvement, was that I was going around with an actor who said I had to take the class because dancing purged the soul. He said you could go to dance class with a hangover or the flu or suicidally depressed, and after an hour and a half of hard work you would feel refreshed and

elated. Even the flu would be gone. He said the only
thing better than a ballet class was two ballet classes
in a row. I settled for one a day, Beginners, and it
was there I first saw Melba.

She was the ugliest girl I had ever seen in my life.
She was so ugly she fascinated me. I would get the
place behind her at the bar so I could stare at her in
the mirror in front of us. She was very thin and all
muscle, with an enormous pouting mouth and sharp
monkey eyes. She wore a bright red leotard, and all
her hair was up in rollers under what looked like a
mobcap. The floppy brim of this grotesque headgear
hid her eyebrows, but flipped up on the sides so her
ears could protrude. She looked like that chimp they
used to dress up to go on television in the mornings.
I wondered who she was. I stared at her every day,
and in the dressing room I looked at her open purse,
her clothes, searching for more clues about her.

She seemed trying to make herself ugly, as if it
was part of the discipline of study. She was not a
particularly good dancer, but she worked hard. She
never spoke to anyone and no one spoke to her.
Every day when ballet class was over she took a
shower, dried herself with a towel marked *Plaza
Hotel,* put on the tightest slacks and the tightest
shirt in New York, yanked them both together with
a heavy leather belt, straightened the mobcap, slung
her canvas bag over her shoulder, and loped to the
elevator.

One day I couldn't stand it any more; there was

no one in the dressing room, so I spoke to her. What does one girl say to another when they are total strangers? It's easy—I complimented her on the hat I hated and asked where she had gotten it. She said it was very old, that she had bought it either in California or Boston or Chicago, she forgot which. Her speech was a little affected but her voice was humorous, as if she was deciding how much she could let go.

I said it was clever of her to set her hair while she was in dance class, since the heat made my hair so stringy. She said that was the only time she ever got. Besides, she said, what difference did it make if you wore rollers and a hat in dance class and looked ugly, because there was no such thing as Ugly, and besides, what mattered when you were dancing was your soul. She added emotionally that dancing was just like life and the only thing that should matter in life was your soul and not external things. Then she said if I was going to the East Side she could give me a lift because she had borrowed somebody's Cadillac convertible.

In the elevator she told me her name was Melba Toast.

"Melba Who?"

"I'm a stripper. You have to have a name like that when you're a stripper—it has to be an object or an idea. I'm very thin, so when I first started working they named me Melba Toast, the skinniest stripper in America. In Chicago I jumped out of a dietetic cake at a Shriners' Club dinner. In L.A. I made a movie, but it was never released. It will be someday, though. But right now I'm giving it all up to study seriously to be a good dancer."

"Oh," I said, wondering why she felt called upon to give Instant Credits.

The borrowed convertible was gleaming like wet gold in the afternoon sun. It had pearlescent plastic seat covers and looked as if it belonged to a gangster. Melba had parked it next to an expired parking meter and there was a ticket tucked under the windshield wiper. A young motorcycle cop was just leaving.

"Excuse me, Officer," Melba said. "Officer . . ."

He looked up. Her voice had suddenly changed; it was the voice of the wronged princess, Ophelia when Hamlet tells her to get to a nunnery—*Yes, my lord.*

"Officer, was that a ticket you were writing?"

The cop stared at her. Her blouse, I noticed, was unbuttoned down to the leather belt, and she wasn't as skinny as I had thought. "I'm terribly sorry," Melba went on in that voice. "Was I parked overtime?"

"You sure were," he said. "You never put any money in this meter at all."

She turned and looked at me as if I were the princess's royal purse carrier and had forgotten my duties. "I'm terribly sorry," Melba said. Her accent became almost British. "My friend was feeling ill and

I took her upstairs to a doctor. I suppose I must have forgotten."

The cop looked at me for the first time. If not actually sick I certainly looked peculiar. "This your friend here?"

"It was only the heat," Melba said graciously. "We just drove here from California and she's very tired. We came right to the doctor. We haven't even unpacked."

He looked at the license plate. "California in this heat," he said. "Quite a trip."

"Yes, and we don't know anybody."

There was a flicker of interest on his face. He was about twenty-two and not bad looking. "Well," he said, "you'll want to look around."

"We're looking forward to it."

"Where are you staying?" he asked, looking at her blouse. Melba was looking at the parking ticket.

"If you have something to write it on I'll give you our phone number."

He pulled the parking ticket from under the windshield wiper and tore it in half. "Seeing as you're strangers in town, and it was only five minutes . . ." He poised his pencil over the torn ticket.

"Thank you, Officer. Thank you."

"Where you girls staying?"

"The Barbizon Hotel for Women," Melba said. "My name's Miss Lamont." We got into the car. "And what's yours, when you call?"

He told her, smiling greedily. We all smiled and

waved to each other as Melba and I drove off to the East Side.

"He was a nice boy," she said. "Too bad."

I THINK it is here I should mention that in life I am a natural-born accomplice. I was the kid whose mother was always saying, "You wouldn't be so bad if it wasn't for that Annie!" Or that Bella or that Carol or on through the alphabet, whoever had a scheme to stir up mischief. Left to myself I am rather a sulker. When I'm depressed I sit home and don't call anybody. I'm not one of those advanced cases who, when you call them, won't go out because they're depressed, but unlike Melba I never have the strength to take the initiative. I never enter contests, buy raffles, or get up early to go to sales. In fact, it is my secret phobia that I never go into stores. I am one of the last surviving mail-order shoppers in New York City—I send away from the ad in the paper. Luckily, I am a perfect size 8 (I told you before, I look like Anybody), and since my taste does not run to sequin-encrusted mermaid sheaths (except secretly) I have no alteration problem. I hated to talk to strangers until the second year of my analysis, and even now I don't really like it very much. Before I entered analysis I couldn't even order a cheese sandwich at the counter at Schrafft's in rush hour because I could never talk up loud enough to get the counter boy's attention. This, of course, is very destructive for a would-be actress, who has to be nice and charming to all sorts of strangers, most of whom are against her from the start, sight unseen, because they've already seen fifty of her twins.

The first few times I went to be interviewed, just to see if I could *read* for a part, I spoke so softly that three producers decided I was a member of the Actors Studio, a misapprehension they probably have to this day. Actually, I could never be a member of the Actors Studio because I would die of fright before I got to the audition. I'm good with soap and floor wax because I genuinely hate those advertising people. I mean, I loathe them. When I rehearse for one of those tweed-suited female cretins who says, "No, Anne Boleyn has to have a Midwestern twang because most of our viewers do," I could punch her. Disrespect is wonderful armor for the shy. The more I hate those people the more jobs I get. What worries me is the day I get well adjusted and unshy and learn to live with them in tolerance, and then I will develop stage fright and won't get any jobs at all. There must be a limit to self-understanding, I feel.

The reason I became an actress is because I wanted people to adore me. I can say this with perfect honesty because I have known it ever since I was a fat, shy four-year-old and the damned two-year-old next door beat me up. I don't share the fantasy of many actresses that playing a part liberates me from my real self; my egotism prevents this. Rather, I feel that every part I play is secretly just like me. My doctor calls this a Weak Ego, but he says it's extremely useful so I plan to keep it.

I don't have any theatrical vices like heavy drinking or nymphomania with Younger Men, but I have a weakness for gooey desserts which I have to watch at all times if only to keep the same costume from fitting day to shooting day, and I have food dreams instead of sex dreams, which someone told me means I am repressed. I think it means I am hungry when I go to sleep. I was overweight in college and got good marks and let boys get only to a certain point with me, out of modesty rather than morals, because I was sure if they ever got a good look at my real body they would run away. After college I fell in love with a man who told me to go on a diet, and I did, and got thin, and began a life of discreet sin like everybody else. You see, I am a follower: first You-Wouldn't-Be-Bad-If-It-Wasn't-For-Annie, then the dieting for my paramour, and then the ballet lessons. Between the dieting and the ballet there was one who told me I dressed like my mother in LaPointe, Michigan, which indeed I did, since she mailed me all my clothes from the Bon Ton Shoppe in LaPointe, and he made me get all new clothes and change my hair style. I seem to appeal to Napoleons, particularly weak ones, who know an accomplice when they see one.

This may be due to an idea I have that women are happiest when they are passive. I don't mean dust

23

mops, but I think women should be influenced by the men they love—it makes both of them happier. Of course, women who are influenced a great deal by men are generally influenced somewhat by everybody, even children and other women, which may be one of the reasons Melba latched on to me as a special friend. She needed someone who was a Nice Girl but totally amenable, and because I had gone to college she seemed to get the idea I was an intellectual. Melba herself had gone to college (I don't remember whether or not she graduated), but she seemed to have escaped entirely without an education. Her passion for Zen came later. In all the time I have known her I never asked her what she majored in, but I secretly enjoy the idea that it was surf-boarding. I can just see her poring over the college catalogues, saying, "That one looks like a gas, you can major in Deep Breathing!" Or picking the one that shows a photograph of the freshman class in Scarlett O'Hara dresses getting ready for the Orange Blossom Queen contest. All this while I was dutifully looking for a school that gave you liberal arts plus drama, and would take someone with my average.

As a matter of fact, maybe she didn't go to college at all, maybe she just says she did because it's part of the image. Like all the things about her, you're never quite sure unless you get documentary proof, and Melba always has documentary proof, including three driver's licenses from three different states, gotten over a period of six years, all of which list her age as twenty-one. She would rather go to a new state and take a new driver's test than let anybody know she is getting older. She's getting to look like a pretty beat-up twenty-one, and she may be an insecure prevaricator, but she certainly is a good driver.

This turned out to be unexpectedly convenient for me on one occasion, when she made a point of showing her driver's license to a young millionaire we were with; then he assumed that if she was twenty-one and looked so sophisticated I must be the same age or even younger—but those things don't matter, do they, unless you're very silly, or an actress, or unmarried, and I'm all three. But I'm getting ahead of my story. I want to go back to right after we met in ballet class, after that first afternoon with the traffic cop.

Other friends were in the habit of going out for a Coke after class, but Melba was not like that. "Come with me," she would say, and it would be an evening. "You have nothing else to do," she would say sternly, as she led me to some stranger's penthouse. There she would stack records on the hi fi, raid the refrigerator (which contained nothing but some splits of champagne and a TV dinner, because it would be a bachelor's penthouse), pour me a drink, make numerous phone calls, and stop me every time I tried to go.

"What else have you got to do? You're just going to go home and get depressed."

"My friend might call," I lied.

"Leave this number with your service." And she

would already be calling my service, leaving the message, in the affected but conspiratorial tones an ex-working girl takes on with one who is still silly enough to be toiling. "Thank you very much, dear. 'Night, now."

All Melba's friends' bachelor apartments were the same: the kind of apartment that is decorated by a woman for a man, and is not seen by the man until the day he moves in and can't find his own dishwasher. Everything was very big, very modern, like the exaggerated set of *Pal Joey*. The lamps were four feet tall and hideous, the ashtray (he didn't smoke, of course) the size of a pre-Columbian sacrificial bowl and just as stony. There had to be red wall-to-wall carpet, the kind you twisted your ankle on unless you took off your shoes. The view of the New York skyline for which the tenant was paying a fortune was always obscured by beaded curtains, or perhaps cut-out replicas of the walls of the Taj Mahal—the up-to-the-minute adaptation of last decade's Shoji screens. There was always a little extravagant touch, like having all the closets lined with priceless wedding sari material, the closets in which he would file his two hundred suits.

By the time whoever he was returned from wherever he was making his fortune, a party usually was in full cry—Melba arguing with the delivery boy from the delicatessen who wanted cash, several bewildered playboy friends of the bachelor, who were not sure why they were invited, the real Miss Lamont from the Barbizon, who was seventeen and crying in a corner because she had taken her first Miltown, the inevitable married man with a diamond ring on his pinkie, who was off to Hialeah the next day and wanted to take all of us as his guests, and me, trying to find some place to hide my filthy leotard.

"How did you get in?" he would ask her. "You didn't have a key."

"I left the door open when I left for class," Melba would say calmly. "Pay this man from the delicatessen, and give him a big tip, he's been waiting an hour."

It was then, at that mysterious moment, that a strong man turned into a mass of mashed potatoes in front of my very eyes. I still can not get used to it and it still upsets me, but it always happened. The rich bachelor, who really was not bad looking if he would go to a gym more often, would reach for his wallet, pay and tip the delivery boy, smile weakly, and then rush downstairs to park his car because Melba had invariably parked it in a bus stop.

When he returned, dinner would be on the table, and everyone would sit down. His Christmas gift caviar and pickled mushrooms would be the vegetable along with the pastrami sandwiches and champagne. He would sit down with his guests, and while we dined he would speak longingly of marlin fishing, of the Greek islands, of Las Vegas. He would plan a trip out loud. It was his escape. As always, Melba would eat nothing. She would talk of an engagement she might take to strip in Las Vegas while he was there.

As soon as dinner was over there was a party Melba wanted us all to go to, or a nightclub she had read about which we must all discover. If we did not have the proper clothes it was all right—she would improvise. She would spend an hour in the bathroom doing her makeup while we all sat around, all strangers, trying to talk to one another, wondering why we were there, remembering that we had no place else to be. The married man would eventually excuse himself and go home to his wife and his packing, after handing his business card to Melba through the half-open bathroom door. She was undoubtedly initialing it with a *W.S.*, and possibly a *T.* for Travel.

"I wanted a quiet evening at home," our host would murmur, "I didn't expect this."

"Don't be an old bore," Melba would say. "Live for the moment." And we would find ourselves in the elevator, an extra split in our hands for the cab ride.

"Isn't she marvelous?" the bachelor-victim-host would say to me as we alighted at some other modern new building. "Isn't she amazing?" And what I couldn't understand was that he really meant it—he admired her.

A week later he would be out of her life, but she always had a kiss-off gift: a stole, a set of luggage, her bills paid, or a string of pearls. And she had the phone numbers of ten of his friends, men who were less reluctant to live for the moment than he. I would console myself at the analyst's by saying that he had been a masochist, a victim, and even a bore. And yet when, six months later, Melba had appendicitis, it was he who re-entered her life to pay her hospital bill, to send her daily red roses, to drive her home. Old masochists never die, they don't even fade away if you play your cards right. . . .

I must add here, before this story becomes too incredible, that Melba had two faces. There was the ballet class one, which was sheer monkey, and there was the nightclub one, which was French film star. She was carefully blonde, carefully tousled, and the longest pair of false eyelashes in the world swept mothlike over her cheeks. The pouting mouth was lustrous, the skin flawlessly painted, and her body was obviously sketched by an artist for *Playboy* before she was born to fit into it. Her clothes were ridiculous because they had no style at all, they simply clung. Men did not find this ridiculous. Many a drink was spilled in many a restaurant when Melba left her table to cross the room to make a phone call. Every nice little boy who grew up thinking a whore looked a certain way, never knowing that a true call girl is as chic as his own sister, went right back to his sixteen-year-old fantasies when he saw Melba's body in a knitted dress.

But she was something even more lethal because

she was so unbelievably corny—she was the whore with the heart of gold. She wept easily, she read Zen, and she had swung with people they admired. If you spoke of having babies her eyes would fill with tears, hinting of a mysterious past and a wistfully longed-for future. She was homeless, penniless, desperate and inexhaustible. She gave them her weaknesses for solace while she played on theirs. I couldn't help it, I was jealous of her, I was.

I had known Melba for about two years when she called me up one night and told me that she had changed her life. She now had a real boyfriend, she was in love.

"He's one of the ten wealthiest bachelors in America, he has a house in Palm Beach and an apartment in New York, he's very famous, we go out with *everybody*. . . ." Nowhere had she said he was nice, but I guess that was love for Melba. She did add that he was sexy and good-looking. She invited me over to meet him.

They were sharing an extraordinary triplex apartment in a beautiful part of town. He was not in the least sexy or good-looking; in fact, he was almost grotesque. But what Melba had somehow forgotten to mention was that he was one of the nicest people I had ever met. I felt shy when I entered the overpowering room, and ten minutes later I was curled up on the velvet couch with my shoes off, talking to him about the old neighborhood where we had grown up. There is an alchemy about sharing an

30

urban middle-class background; people admit it to each other like an old disease, and then they love each other for it, imagining they have known each other for years. It's what Melba would call doing the *haimish* bit.

The biggest surprise, however, was Melba. She was as silent as a Japanese wife. She listened—she did not fake it—and she made coffee at midnight and set out little cakes to go with it.

"I'm glad you and Melba are such good friends," he told me while she was in the kitchen. "I always think a girl who has girlfriends is a nice person."

"Oh?"

"Melba talks about you all the time. She says you're her best friend."

"I'm very flattered," I said. It was not really a lie.

"Most girls don't like other girls," he said.

Here I am, I thought, Miss Wholesome, the friend for all seasons.

"You know, she surprises me," he went on quietly. "I had heard such stories about her, how she was such a kook—wild, you know—and she's not like that at all. She's really a little house cat. She likes to stay home, she's a good cook. . . ."

Maybe, I thought, she has found peace at last. I mean, even if a man is one of the ten richest bachelors in America, that doesn't make him all bad.

I visited them often, and Melba *was* like a little house cat—immaculate, silent, soft. She washed the dishes, sponged the drainboard, made the beds, pruned the plants on their terrace, and purred when she spoke to him. They had cat nicknames for each other. It was a little sickening, but then, so are some marriages.

The only wild party she ever gave while she lived with him was perfectly excusable, because it was to mark their first anniversary together. It is true that she could not pay for all of it herself—in fact, he ended up paying for five cases of imported champagne, three maids, a bartender, a piano player, her hairdressing bill (four months overdue anyway) and a seventy-pound memorial cake that she jumped out of in memory of her act, scattering butter-cream icing all over his Aubusson carpet. But the party was a sentimental gesture, and all his friends complimented them on it.

Their first anniversary party was such a great success that nothing could really be better; it was, therefore, the beginning of the end for them. People should never be too splashy about landmarks in love; love should drift on, as Melba used to say, moment to moment. There is something too final about a celebration, for we are used to them: marriages, bar mitzvahs, golden weddings, wakes. A ceremony signals a pinnacle reached, a moment that will never be reached again. She should not have given that party to commemorate a mere one year in sin, she should have waited for something more tangible.

Of course, it could have been her skittishness that ended their romance, and the way Melba always tells every story, it always is. What happened, as nearly as I could piece it out, was that she was suffering from infected tonsils and adenoids and the doctor said she had to have them removed. Melba said she did not want to go to a strange surgeon, she wanted to go home to her parents. It was the first anyone had heard of her parents, but I suppose she must have had them, she was not sprung full-grown from that dietetic cake. Besides, she said, her uncle back home was the best throat specialist in the Midwest. So her lover gave her a thousand dollars, a packet of throat lozenges, an airline ticket, and a fond goodbye kiss, and she gave him a promise that she would write every day and return in three weeks. She did not return for six months.

Instead of Uncle Doc's, she went to Hollywood, where she spent the thousand dollars on a new wardrobe, a room in the Beverly Hills Hotel, and a rented Corvette. Soothed by these emollients, her throat trouble went away. The adenoids made her speaking voice more alluring, and she was "discovered" by some little rat who called himself a talent scout, and she made another movie. This movie was never released either, for reasons of avant-gardism or something more simple, but the money was gone, Melba was meeting people, and she forgot to write home at all. She danced till dawn in nightclubs, she learned to water ski, she dyed her hair red, and finally, she came back to New York.

When she got there she discovered that the triplex

apartment had been sublet, her millionaire had moved away (no forwarding address, unlisted phone) and her clothes had been stored in the basement. Unkindest cut of all, he had stolen her electric clock (which she had stolen from someone else). Through one of his friends she soon located him, and wrote him the following note:

TIGERCAT—

I can't understand why you are angry, since all I wanted to do was follow my chosen career. You have always encouraged me in the arts, and it is small of you to be jealous now. I didn't write or call because I'm not a verbal person. Besides, you never really loved me. You *know* you never loved me. You never loved anyone. Think about that with your conscience. Anyway, I still love you as much as I always did.

Yours, as ever,

PUSSYCAT

P.S. It was stinking of you to steal my electric clock, when you damn well have six of your own and all of them better than mine.

When he received this letter he telephoned her, at a girlfriend's where she was recovering from her broken heart, and told her he was going to try his best to forget her as quickly as he could. Melba replied that he had also stolen her bathmat (which it happened she had stolen from me). He said he would buy her a new bathmat and a new electric clock, since they had been misplaced in the moving, and Melba replied that she no longer wanted anything from him since he was incapable of love.

After that she went on a rampage of dating, punctuated by evenings sobbing about her lost love and how beautiful it had been. Her version of the story became more touching as time went on; finally it was that he had proposed and she had run away out of fear that she could never be a proper wife until she settled her psychological problems. She talked a great deal about the art movie, although no one I know of ever saw it in a public place, and sometimes I wonder if she was ever in it at all, or if it even existed, or if everyone would have been better off if it had not existed after all.

As for Tigercat, he was the only man I ever met who was vindictive about Melba, and who actually tried to make her sound like the rejected one in their romance. He spread it around nastily that the thousand dollars was kiss-off money, her trip was a ruse, and his new apartment was his escape. I'm certain no one will ever know for sure, least of all the two of them.

One of the strangest things about Melba is her pride. I am not sure whether it is pride, lack of pride, or an extraordinary confidence in the kindness of unreality. A few months after they broke up she met Tigercat accidentally in a nightclub, and fled in tears. A month after that she was telephoning him happily long distance, from someone's apartment, to congratulate him on a financial coup of his she had read about in the newspaper. They were both cordial, and she said she hoped to see him when she came back to New York, and he said he hoped so too, although they were both lying. I mean, he was lying . . . Melba was telling the truth.

When she came back to New York she began her lunch circuit, a new form of meeting men which she had just discovered. "Between one and three," she told me. "That's when you meet all the attractive men, between one and three."

She chose one of New York's most exclusive and expensive restaurants as her base of operations, and when she could not find a date to bring her there she began to show up alone. The waiters were all used to her; they simply assumed she had been stood up. Often she was joined by a man who had been watching her from the bar; he left a large tip and no one said anything about it.

One afternoon she was unlucky—she met no one and had a large luncheon bill to pay. But Melba calmly and with shaking heart signed the check, and found herself with no references, no bank account, no permanent address, no employment, and a new charge account.

The restaurant was one where you could have a phone brought to the table, which was one of the reasons Melba liked it. I don't think she felt any link to reality unless she had a telephone receiver in her hand. I had quit my hopeless romance with my actor and my ballet classes, and when I was not working, which was often that year, I slept late so the day would go away. Around one-thirty my phone would ring, and it would be Melba.

"Get up and come over," she would command. "I'm with two charming men."

"Are they attractive?"

"Terribly attractive, and sexy, too. Come right over."

"Are they married?"

"Hurry up, we're not going to sit here all afternoon."

"They're right there with you, right? So that means you can't talk, but they're not very attractive, and they are married, but they're from out of town and they want to see everything."

"Mmm." That meant yes.

"It will take me too long to get dressed," I would say, and go back to sleep.

Half an hour later the phone would ring again. "Come on! Yours is divine."

Mine! He was mine already. And he was on the phone. He always sounded frightened, tentative, and a little too intimate for comfort. "Why don't you join us later for cocktails?" he would say. "Melba tells me you're charming."

That always infuriates me. I mean, I'm supposed to join this stranger for drinks because *he's* been told *I'm* charming. Not because I want to meet him, but because I've passed the test. And I usually go, because I am lonely, and Melba is funny, and I want to see the festivities in their full, total, horrible boredom and humiliation so I'll know what I've been jealous of all these years.

This particular evening it was arranged that "mine" would pick me up at my apartment and we would join Melba and "hers" at his hotel. I was glad I was living in a walkup with no doorman or elevator man to give me a fishy look, because as soon as the long black car with the blue-tinted windows drew up to the curb and the glittering, pomaded, scented, talcumed old man stepped out, I knew I was in for it. He even had a hat on; I knew he always wore a hat, and I knew he was surprised and disappointed that I didn't look or dress like Melba.

We went to a very expensive tourist trap with fountains and colored lights and waiters who whisk away the ashtray every time you flick one ash into it. The plans had been changed at the last minute, Melba and her date would join us here. They were late.

My date had a star sapphire ring on his pinkie instead of a diamond, with star sapphires at his cuffs and another pinning his tie. We smiled at each other and he said he supposed I would have champagne because Melba always had champagne, and I said I would have Scotch. He looked at me a little embarrassed and said I was younger than he had expected. I said, how old did he think I was, and he said twenty-one, and then I really knew he was old, because I am twenty-six.

We sipped our drinks for a while in silence, and then he took out his wallet and asked me if I would like to see pictures of his children. I thought, Oh, maybe he's trying to be my friend, thank God; and I looked at the pictures. He had a son and a daughter just a little younger than I. I said how pretty they were, as if we were discussing baby pictures, and then I knew that we couldn't be friends after all because we were too self-conscious about what we thought we owed each other.

"Melba's always late," I said.

"They're probably in his room, tearing off a fast one," Star Sapphire said smugly. "I wouldn't blame him."

I just kept sitting there, thinking, Oh, shut up, you old goat; but sitting there, which is a problem I have to talk over with my analyst at much greater length.

"If they don't show up soon, would you like to order dinner?" he asked. "It'll serve them right."

"Actually, I have to go home . . . I have to prepare for an audition tomorrow . . . I shouldn't really be out at all. . . ."

They entered the restaurant, waving to us. Melba was wearing a dress I had never seen before, and would never have expected to see on her in any case; it was a very ladylike, elegant dress, and she looked beautiful in it. They said they had been drinking at the hotel, and Star Sapphire gave me a knowing look which I ignored, and we asked for menus.

You know the menus in these places, they're enormous, they look like headstones. Melba propped hers up and whispered to me from behind it, "How do you like my dress?"

"It's gorgeous."

"He bought it for me, just now. Six hundred dollars. I told him we'd be too late if I had to go home to change, and I didn't feel like going out in the same dress I had on all day."

"Six hun——"

"Shh!" She touched her purse, which was on the table. "I have my old dress rolled up in there. His hotel has an arcade of shops. He wanted to buy me a bag to go with it, but I didn't want him to spend any more money."

"You should have let me buy you the purse," her date said. "It was beautiful."

"It was too expensive," Melba said.

"That's what money's for, isn't it?" he said. He seemed in his mid or late thirties, and quite ordinary looking; I couldn't figure out why he felt he had to buy affection. He looked like the kind of man you go to the movies with, and a hamburger later, and then some day you marry. He didn't look like his sand was running out. I couldn't understand him at all.

From the minute he looked at Melba across the table my date had forgotten I existed. He talked to her, he flirted with her, he didn't try to show her baby pictures. When it was time for dessert nobody wanted any but me, and he said I could have it in the nightclub where we were going later, a new nightclub Melba said we mustn't miss.

We walked out to the street. "It's a little large," Melba said, pinching the dress. "I'll have to have it taken in. . . ."

"Don't!" I said. "You'll ruin it."

Star Sapphire had called for his car. "I'm tired," he said. "I don't want to go to a nightclub. I'm going home." He turned to me. "Would you like me to drop you off?"

"It's the beginning of the evening!" Melba cried. She took me by the arm and pulled me to the shelter of a doorway next to the restaurant. My date had already climbed into his car and was sitting at the wheel, the door open.

"Listen," Melba whispered fiercely, "you're my friend, you *can't* leave me with him. I don't want to be alone with him. He thinks I'm going to screw him for his dress. Well, I'm not."

"Just tell him you thought it was a present and thank him," I said. "I can't hang around, he'll get mad."

"I don't care if he gets mad. You stay!"

"Going or coming?" Star Sapphire asked, looking at me with tired hatred.

"Spoilsport!" Melba said. "Party pooper! Don't be a drag. Come with us."

Star Sapphire slammed his door and drove away. I felt tired and lonely and embarrassed—I had done everything I had been brought up not to do, except for the one thing that would have made it all right, and there was no way to communicate with these people or make them see that I was a person or even that they were persons, that you didn't have to play a game with rules every night, that some nights you could just exist. They had never known any other way.

"You should have gone with him," Melba's date said.

"I asked her to stay," Melba said.

"Well, whose date is she, his or yours?"

"Hers," I said nastily.

Melba choked over her laughter. He started to walk ahead. "Where can we get a drink?" he asked.

We went to a small bar around the corner, where we seemed to be the only patrons. Melba's date had two quick drinks and suddenly became very depressed.

"I hate New York," he said. He put his head down on the bar. "People are unfriendly in New York. They're out to cheat you. I'm leaving here tomorrow and I'm never coming back."

"What do you do in . . . um . . . where you come from?" I asked, trying to make conversation. Melba had decided not to talk at all and was looking through her address book and humming.

"I go steady. I go out with my steady girl for dinner at my favorite restaurant. I work. That's all. It's a good life."

"Have you known Mel long?"

"I met her once before, last trip. She was different then, I thought. She was nicer. She's changed."

"I haven't changed," Melba said. "You have no perception. What do you expect from me? I'm a human being, I have my problems. You think you are the only person who is entitled to have problems?"

"Oh, why don't you go home?" he said to me.

I stood up and put on my coat. Melba got up too and pulled him to his feet. "We're going," she said. "Pay the man."

Melba and I stood on the curb while he hailed a taxi. "I'm going to make him drop me off, and then he can drop you off," she told me. "You'll be safe with him."

"Sure, he'll only murder me."

"No he won't, he's drunk. I didn't ask him to buy me this dress—he insisted. I'll fix him. I'm going to Tiffany's tomorrow and buy him a pair of jade cuff links. I'll send them to him at home. They'll be for the dress. I'll show him."

"You may change his whole life."

"Mmm. On the other hand, I can buy the cuff links wholesale and put them in a Tiffany box. Do you have an old Tiffany box you can give me? He'll never know the difference."

"Why don't you just mail him the dress?"

"It was a present."

The three of us got into the cab, and although it was out of the way he insisted that we stop at Melba's address first. She jumped out of the cab, and he jumped after her, thrusting a folded bill into my hand.

"Go on, driver," he said, in a tone of such firm command that the cab was moving almost before he was out of it. I looked through the rear window and saw Melba peck him swiftly on the lips, and then I saw her doorman come out and I knew she had won. I looked at the bill in my hand and saw that it was a dollar.

I don't know why, but I felt oddly disappointed, as if for this one unreal night I, too, had become a cab-fare girl, and should have opened my palm to find it contained a fifty.

The next morning Melba called me. "You certainly beat it in a hurry," she said. She was not angry.

"I couldn't help it . . . what could I do, break his arm?"

"Ha! You just wanted to keep that ten."

"What ten?"

"The ten dollars he gave you. I know."

"He gave me a dollar!"

"You're kidding."

"No, I'm not. He gave me a dollar, I swear."

"A dollar!" Melba said indignantly. "Charlie Cheap. I'll never go out with him again."

Here is the point where I should go into a treatise on the perversion of values and how bad company wrecks your soul, but the truth is that when it's happening you never notice it. You hardly even feel guilty. You just don't believe any of it is real. It's all like a game, or a play, and the people in it are going to disappear soon and everything will be all right. You're not you, even though the streets you walk through are familiar because you walked through them in happier and sadder times when you were you. And you know you'll walk through them again when you are you again, and all that is happening right now is going to be a funny story you'll remember, a little ashamed, a little incredulous, but busy going wherever you are going. And that's all.

It is still a big step between being willing to go with the rules and knowing what they are. Melba still had the capacity to surprise me. A month later she mentioned casually that she had been lunching alone at her favorite restaurant: "Just a couple of drinks and a main course, and they hit me with this twenty-eight-dollar bill, and I had to call Lem at his office to come over and rescue me."

Lem—Star Sapphire! The way she dropped his real name so calmly froze me in my tracks. I realized she had been seeing him, that she actually even liked him, or at least, that he had become one of her group. "You'll remember," she told me, "I always thought he was attractive."

I think I began to become a little less jealous of her that day; although something in me still urged that perhaps Star Sapphire had been attractive, that I had allowed myself to be adversely influenced by the triteness of the very things Melba liked. So what if he was too old—my mother wasn't watching behind the banquette. So what if he thought he had to buy my time—Melba wanted to sell hers. You couldn't call him a dirty old man, he was an expensively clean old man, and he hadn't done anything more offensive than be bored and be boring. Don't sit under the apple tree with anyone else but me, and you'll eat wormy apples the rest of your life. So when she called me up a week later and said to meet her and a new friend back at her favorite restaurant, I put on my sexiest dress and went over.

This new man, she told me on the phone, she had met in the oddest way. He had telephoned her to say that he had found her name and phone number scribbled on a scrap of paper in his wallet, and he supposed they had met at a cocktail party some time before when he had been high, since he could not remember when or how they had met or when she had given him her number, and neither could Melba. But they both agreed it was worth a look, and after several changes of plan they finally agreed on the tryst I was now about to attend as chaperone. Melba had a habit of saying very firmly that she had a previous engagement for dinner with a girlfriend, and if the man wanted to see her he would have to take them both to dinner. The man always agreed. He probably thought out of two one would be promising, and that any girl who was so devoted to her girlfriend

46

couldn't be all bad. There is a little of Tigercat in most men.

When I arrived at the restaurant, a man who looked like Star Sapphire's grandfather (one of Ripley's wonders if he could still be alive) was waiting nervously in front of the checkroom.

"I don't know how to explain this," he said, "but your friend left."

He was so upset I agreed to have a drink with him while he explained what had happened. He was known there, and evidently either rich or celebrated, because we were ushered to one of the best tables.

"I picked her up in my limousine," he said, "and she had called another girlfriend of hers, a model, because she was afraid you weren't going to show up. She said this model had just come in from out of town and wanted to see her or something, I forget exactly. Anyway, we were coming here, the three of us, and suddenly Melba leaned forward and said to my driver, 'Drive past Forty-fifth Street.' There was a play opening and Melba said she had an old boyfriend in it. I told her it was silly, that it's impossible to get opening night tickets ten minutes before curtain time, but she said to leave everything to her. We stopped at the theater and Melba said to me, 'Give me a hundred dollars,' so I did, and she went into the lobby. She came out five minutes later waving two opening night orchestra tickets, and told me she had bought them from someone in the lobby for fifty dollars apiece. Well, there were three of us with her

47

girlfriend being there, and only two tickets, so Melba said she and her girlfriend would go to the show and I should come here and wait for you so you wouldn't be stood up. They're going to come here after the play and join us for dinner."

"They're never coming back," I said.

"Of course they are."

I looked at him—the white talcumed jowls, the white-on-white brocade tie, the seven-hundred-dollar suit, the white little hands, all the mortality of him, the same way he would look some day for his first-class funeral, a sad, frightening, vindictive, lonely little man.

"Do you always carry around stacks of hundred-dollar bills?" I asked. He didn't answer me.

"How did you meet Mel?" I asked.

"A friend gave me her number."

"Who?"

"I don't remember."

"Why did you let them leave you like that?"

"She wanted to see the play," he said.

"What makes you think she'll come back?"

"She'll come back," he said calmly. "What would you like to drink?"

If I'm going to be like Melba, I'll live like Melba, I thought; and so I ordered champagne, but I must have done it wrong because no one brought the bottle to the table for me to inspect the label, and the headwaiter poured a glassful from an already opened magnum that looked half empty and tasted sour.

"Melba didn't tell you, but I have a date later," I said. "I'll just keep you company for a while and then I have to go."

"You have to eat dinner," he said.

"I'll have to eat later."

"I'm going to order dinner," he said. "I don't like to eat alone."

I ordered the kind of dinner Melba would have ordered: lobster cocktail, pheasant under glass, hearts of palm salad—and I choked on every bite of it. Now I realized why she never ate anything when she went out to dinner. He ate the calm, spare meal of someone who must watch his heart, and he told me that he had been recently divorced from his third wife, an alcoholic, and that he was lonely. It is a terrible thing to be lonely with someone else who is lonely too and to know that there is not one single thing either of you can do to make it different.

"Do you live in an apartment or a hotel?" I asked.

"An apartment. I own the building."

"That's convenient."

"I don't know why I bought it," he said, bored and weary. "We'll go up there afterward for a drink."

"We have to wait for Melba."

"I'll leave the address with the headwaiter."

"Listen," I said, reduced to a seventeen-year-old girl again, idiotic, forgetting my fictitious late date, forgetting everything, "I'm a friend of Melba's but I'm not like her."

"What do you mean?"

"I mean . . ." I looked into his innocent hard eyes. "I mean—she looks kind of sexy, the way she dresses and all, and you might get the wrong impression about her, but I mean . . ."

His eyes had died years ago; what he looked out of was a pair of electronic marbles, measuring, counting, clicking out the result irrevocably; once the numbers have been fed into the machine the result is predetermined, you cannot change the robot, you cannot cheat IBM.

"I'm not fooled by sexy-looking girls like Melba," he said. "I know that it's the little drab mice like you who get all the goodies. Isn't that true?"

"What are the goodies?"

"Sex," he said, and smiled.

There is a moment of decision in every girl—no, maybe in every person regardless of sex or age or intention—when reality snaps off; what Melba means by "the moment." It may be only a moment, or it may be a month or a year, but it is a self-contained moment with its own logic. It is the logic of nightmare, but just like a nightmare it follows through to the end, making its own kind of sense. Maybe it's the moment when there are too many answers and the choice is too difficult, or the moment when reality has been strained so far that unreality turns into hypnotism. I don't know, but I had one of those moments, and so I did not get up and walk out or slap him or cry or faint or go into the ladies' room to throw up, I just drank my demitasse and powdered my nose and said it was time for me to meet my date. I was calm and he was calm. He looked at his wrist watch and paid the check. We walked out of the restaurant together, and at the front door he stopped to murmur to the captain that if Miss Toast and her friend came looking for him to tell them we had gone back to his apartment.

Then we walked to the street where his limousine was waiting, we got into it, and he dropped me off at a restaurant a few blocks away where I told him my date was waiting. Then he drove away. I waited a few minutes until I was sure he was gone, and then I got a cab and went home.

The only thing I thought when I got home was that it was very insulting to be called a drab little mouse, and maybe I was funny looking or getting old? I looked into the mirror a long time.

I never mentioned any part of the evening to my analyst, because from that moment until just now when I have recalled it, it never happened; except between me and Melba, and that's different.

A few days afterward when I spoke to her again on the phone she told me I certainly had my nerve going off to her date's apartment and leaving her and her friend sitting there starving to death. "We didn't even have dinner!" she said indignantly.

"I didn't think you'd come back."

"Where did you think I was going to go? I was looking forward to a nice dinner after the play."

"I didn't go to his apartment."

"The captain said you went to his apartment."

"I can't understand where he got that idea," I said. "I can't understand it at all. How could you stick me with that terrible old man? That's the last time I ever meet you and one of your dates."

"He wasn't so terrible," Melba said. "Didn't you like his limo?"

"He said I was a drab little mouse."

She laughed. "I thought you'd like to get out and have a nice dinner. If you'd come earlier you could have gone to the play, too. It was marvelous, the best play I ever saw. You have to go see it. Go right away, I mean it. You'll flip!"

She went on for ten minutes about the play, and about the theater in general—Melba thinks she knows a lot about the theater—and then she said I should go back to dance class, and before I knew it the subject of the terrible old man was closed.

Except that a month later I discovered she had been going to the racetrack with the terrible old man every Saturday after that, and they had won fourteen thousand dollars on the double-triple or some such thing, and he had split it with her. For some reason I wasn't jealous at all. I think I probably would have been stupid enough to pay taxes on it, had I won seven thousand dollars, even in the line of combat.

During the time I have known her, a period of

some four years, Melba and I have had several long midnight talks, the kind girls have in school dormitories wearing flannel nightgowns and slipper socks —about Love, Parents, Life and The Future. Melba's parents were divorced when she was a baby, so she never really knew her father while she was growing up, but then when she did grow up and became more interesting or less frightening, her father took an interest in her again and they became rather friendly. In a way there seemed something unhealthy about their friendship: he had met her for the first time, so to speak, as an adult, they were equals except that he had the money, and he was anxious to appear young. Melba's father, from what she told me about him, would definitely rate as an S., having been married four or five times, and would have qualified as a W., except that he was paying most of it in alimony. I had learned that her descriptions of men were largely fictitious, and I pictured him as looking like Star Sapphire. I suppose people really don't know their own motivations even when they are so obvious to others as to appear trite. It seemed obvious to me that Melba was trying to get back at her father for deserting her, and that was why she delighted in getting as much as she could from older men, and at the same time she rather liked these men because they did remind her in some way of her father. But then I thought that perhaps Melba knew all this and had invented the father she told me about so that I would "discover" a rationalization for her behavior.

When her father married his fourth or fifth wife Melba was not allowed to attend the ceremony, she told me, because the bride was two years younger than she was. Several months later she told me, delighted, that her father was getting a divorce.

"Now, there's the man for you," she told me. "You're in luck. He's handsome, he's virile, he's wealthy, he loves to travel, he's a swinger, all the chicks are mad for him, and he's getting a divorce. I'll introduce you to him."

"I'll be your stepmother!"

"That's the point. Think of all the charge accounts. . . . I know you'll give me anything I want. You and I will both be rich."

"Why can't you just get him to give you some money, like other girls' fathers do?" I said. "I don't have to marry him."

"He's too busy giving money to all his wives. When it gets around to me he's too poor." She opened her purse and took out a letter. "Here's a letter I got from him a couple of days ago."

DEAR DAUGHTER,

Sorry I haven't written sooner but nothing much is new. Business is keeping me pretty busy, but I went to the track a couple of times and the weather is good. I guess you heard Dolly went to Reno to

get a divorce. This is it. Hope to see you in a month
or two when I come to New York.

Letters from parents who say "Dear Daughter"
and sign themselves "Your Father" or "Your Mother"
always seem very strange to me. Doesn't he remember
his daughter's name? Or is he reminding her (or
himself) of the relationship? And the signature . . .
did he think a simple "Father" would seem too
vague, or too intimate and lacking in respect owed
him? Or maybe that's just the way the lower class
writes letters, or is it the upper class who does? Anyway, no one I know ever did. The letter was written
on motel stationery with a picture of a palm tree on
it, and he had the large sprawling handwriting of a
fourth-grader. The few lines he had written covered
the entire page. On the other hand, maybe he was
just trying to use up space. After all, I don't know
him.

And I never did meet him, either. He was a mystery man, who traveled. I never knew exactly what
he did for a living; one of Melba's boyfriends told
me her father owned a huge housing development,
while another told me he was a bartender. She said
he was neither. I don't know whether I never could
remember what he did, or whether Melba was pur-
posely vague. Or perhaps I wasn't listening. Every
time Melba began on that "Now there's the man for
you" bit about her father I began to blank out from

nervousness. She had accomplished so many of her fantastic wishes that I was afraid she might have, after all, some barbed-wire strength that could turn me into her indulgent stepmother.

Melba never spoke about her mother, except once. She did not seem to bear her mother any particular animosity, nor was she particularly devoted. It was her father who had wounded her, and her father whom she adored.

"I can never find a man who will love me enough," Melba liked to say. "I need a great deal of love because my father deserted me. I've been engaged six times, but I never could go through with it because I knew he didn't have enough love in him."

I had met three out of the six ex-fiancés, and they didn't have enough love in them, all three put together, to keep a goldfish happy. They had, however, shown more kindness and consideration to Melba than they ever had to anyone else, judging from stories I had heard about them. Perhaps it was only because she had asked, when no one else had dared, or because she seemed to inspire this guilt in some men.

She inspired something more than guilt—and I don't mean lust, because people who lust after a stereotype don't know what lust is, only the stereotype of it. What she inspired, I think, was admiration. Melba is a pest about going out to some dumb discotheque to dance all night, but she isn't a pest about her troubles the way most people are. I remember one evening she called me and said calmly, "I've just been sitting here crying."

"Why were you crying?"

"I don't remember . . . my aunt died or something. There must have been some reason. Let's get dressed and go find some action." I knew she didn't have any aunt; that was the same aunt who dies every time you want to stay away from work.

A girlfriend of mine, who knows Melba, once said something that I think sums up the whole attitude people have about her. "If her strap broke at a party and her dress fell down, somebody would throw her a coat. No one would *hand* her a coat, and no one would leave her standing there, but they'd *throw* her a coat. Even just looking at the way she acts every day," my friend said, "people want to throw her a coat."

In real life, a lot of people threw Melba real coats: two minks, a leopard, and a snow fox, whatever that is. Or maybe it was a snow leopard. Melba's titles for her fur coats get grander the rattier the coat gets; I mean the second year around her fox turned into a chinchilla. I will not soon forget the night she tried to go out wearing her mink sweater with her mink coat over it (and a four-dollar skirt she had conned free out of the man who owned the sportswear company). I told her she looked like an ad for a thrift shop.

"Why, too much?"

"Too much and too hot. Your head disappears."

"I'll start a fad."

Fur on fur, the tiny ankles in pointed high-heeled shoes, the tiny face of which nothing could be seen but a tangle of furry red hair with bangs flicked by those long black fake eyelashes, lashes so thick and long you could not look into the eyes beneath, a rich mouth she had turned into an obscene confection with seven layers of parfait-colored lipstick—she looked like the Draw Me girl. She *was* the Draw Me girl! I saw all at once, what I had never seen before because I knew her too well and was still seeing the person on the nights the person disappeared beneath the art. Melba was no fool; she knew scared people don't want to look at other scared people, they want to eat bonbons and play with toys.

It's funny how even at the moment you are discovering how vulnerable somebody is, you can become more jealous of that person because he knew how to fool you. Also, I can tell myself that a girl who has to wear layers of makeup and run to the powder room to comb her hair every half hour is very insecure, but I also know that the end result makes her feel very secure, and so I am jealous of her. I am jealous of her for being able to be happy with so little.

I want to get to the one time Melba mentioned her mother. It was another intolerable August. Melba telephoned me about eight o'clock in the evening, when it had just started to cool off, and said, "Come on over, my mother got me a blind date with two Olympic tennis players."

What mother? It seemed to me then that Melba's whole life was a throwaway line, it went by so fast. "Is your mother in New York?"

"No, no. She met them in Europe and told them to call me when they got here."

"That's a nice mother." What mother? And tennis at the Olympics?

"They must have made a great impression on her, my mother never sends me a guy unless he's good-looking."

Olympic tennis players sounded healthy and wholesome and young. She didn't know their names, but one of them had called her just before she called me and they were coming over that night. Tennis players . . . well, what the hell. I put on the tightest, sexiest black dress I owned, messed up my hair into a facsimile of Melba's and sprayed it stiff to stay that way, doused myself with my heaviest perfume, glued on the false eyelashes that I wear in front of a camera, took a quarter for the ladies' room and a dollar for the cab so she couldn't borrow anything from me, and armed with the *joie de vivre* and desperation of the penniless—a heady feeling I rather liked—I went to Melba's apartment.

She was sitting at the dining area table sipping absinthe and gluing on her eyelashes. I noticed with satisfaction that we looked like sisters, or at least members of the same chorus line.

"You look stunning," she said. "Did you ever have real absinthe? This is smuggled."

The real absinthe was very strong. She was drinking hers straight because the color was prettier, so I did the same.

"Did you eat?"

"No."

"Well, they'll take us out to supper," she said. "They're having dinner with Pancho somebody at his house, and then they'll pick us up at eleven. Meanwhile we can have a snack here."

We looked into the refrigerator and found seven Doggie Bags in various stages of decrepitude, containing Melba's uneaten restaurant leftovers from the past week. "I guess I ought to throw those out," she said, and did. There were also several trays of ice cubes, a lemon, an onion, and a bottle of Instant Cocktail Foam.

We settled for the absinthe, some cookies she said she made herself, and some candy from a gift box. Melba always has candy and flowers on her coffee table, and there is always a half-empty bottle of the best champagne standing next to the unused cutlery. She wandered around the room, perfuming herself from a newly opened two-ounce size of Savage Jasmin, and left the perfume bottle in the middle of the coffee table. There's one thing you have to say for Melba, she makes it easy for a man to know what kind of perfume and champagne to bring.

It was ten-thirty. "I'll call them," she said. "Maybe

they forgot. If they stand us up . . ." Then she sat down again. "That Pancho whatever must have an unlisted number. We'll wait. I hope I didn't scare them by sounding too cold. I said eleven was rather late, and I'd meet them for lunch tomorrow at my usual place."

"That's an expensive restaurant for amateur athletes," I said.

"Oh, it is not. They'll still show tonight. Come on, let's get prepared."

We went into the closet and smoked a joint she had scrounged from some party. She had a solid gold roach holder she said was the kind of present a man gives a girl who has everything.

Then it was eleven o'clock. "How long should we give them before we leave?" she said.

"Half an hour?"

"When we go into the restaurant, where can we say we've been? How about theater? What should we say we've seen?"

"Nobody cares what we've seen," I said. "The waiter isn't going to ask us where we were before."

"We're dressed up . . . we can just say we were at a cocktail party and decided to have dinner."

"Maybe the tennis players will come."

"No, they'll probably call me tomorrow. Besides, if they're late I'd rather not be here."

"Can we go out alone?"

"That's just what I've been asking you," Melba said.

"Well, why not?"

"The evening is young."

"I hate to get all dressed up for nothing."

"Let's go quick, before it gets too late for us to look as if we've just come from theater."

"Why do we have to tell them where we've been?"

"Two girls can go out alone."

"What's open this late is the problem," I said. "And I have to be able to charge it because I have no money."

"I know where we can go free," Melba said. She yanked a last time at her dress, her hair, licked her glistening lips. "The owner always picks up the check for me . . . at least, sometimes. He will if he sees it's just two girls alone. I bring a lot of my dates there—three, four times a week. He'll pick up the check. He knows me."

That sounded less lonely; the fatherly host. What else did we have to do, sit home and get depressed? Go where the action was, find the action, make some action . . . and don't spend any money! It was then I began to feel that odd transference you sometimes get when you have long envied and observed someone else . . . maybe it was only the real absinthe on an empty stomach, or maybe I really was turning into another Melba . . . I looked into the mirror in her lobby. We certainly looked like twins in our uniforms, slinky, faceless, and fuzzy, two sleek little New York ferrets out for a free night on the town.

Melba's doorman straightened, almost saluted. "May I get you a cab?"

"No, thank you, we'll take my car." She turned smartly and walked in the direction of the garage on the corner.

"What car? You didn't tell me you got a . . ."

"Shut up, Brilliant. I didn't want to give him a tip."

She paused for a minute at the garage to exchange advice on the horses with the boy who worked there, and then when the doorman had gone back into the building she smiled goodbye at the boy and pushed me.

"Run!"

We ran around the corner and paused breathlessly on Park Avenue. Melba was scanning the empty cabs as they cruised by. "This one looks like our people," she said. "Run!"

We ran to the taxi and climbed in. When the driver turned to look at us I recognized him from acting class. He was an out-of-work actor who drove a cab nights. I was embarrassed to be the passenger when he was working, as if he had caught me being rich, and I jabbered and giggled and introduced him to Melba, who jabbered and giggled, and when we reached the restaurant he threw the flag and refused to take any money.

"You see?" Melba said. "I told you he looked like our people. Park the cab and come in and have a drink."

"I can't, I haven't got a tie."

"They'll give you one at the coat check."

"Another time," my friend said. He smiled at us like a grownup sending two children off to play, and drove away.

Melba held her head high and walked into the restaurant, conscious that all the men at the bar were looking at her. I held my head the same way, walked the same way, and felt looks I had never felt before. I hoped to God none of them knew me.

"I knew it," Melba whispered as we waited for our table, "this is going to be a lucky night for me. I can feel my luck. I knew it when I found that cabby."

"He was *my* friend!"

"But *I* found him. You were ready to take any cab."

We were ushered to a conspicuous banquette table for two in the Celebrity Room, which differed from the non-celebrity rooms in that it was the only one with people in it. Melba and I were the only un-escorted women. Because it was late there were only a few tables occupied. We looked around the room discreetly.

"It looks dull," Melba said. She ordered champagne and asked for a phone.

The waiter brought the champagne and said that we would have to wait for the telephone because the gentleman in the corner was using it for business. Melba looked with considerable interest at the gentle-man in the corner. He was dining alone. She asked the waiter who he was, but the waiter looked embarrassed and hurried away without answering, so that intrigued both of us. Melba called the captain over, because he knew her, and after a minute or two of happy welcomes she asked him who the man with the phone was. The captain said he was a prominent figure in a current vice trial and would probably be going to jail on Monday and he needed the phone to make some last-minute appeals.

"Just our luck," I said.

"Let's send him a note," Melba said.

"What are you going to tell him?"

"To give us the phone, naturally. Only I'll be nice about it." She got a pad from the waiter and took a pen from her purse. When she opened her purse to get it I noticed about a hundred dollars in twenty-dollar bills.

"If the gangster doesn't give us the phone," I said, "maybe at least he'll send us a drink."

"Don't you know who buys you a drink and who doesn't?" Melba said pityingly.

"He won't?"

"We'll be lucky if we get the phone."

She printed: *Two desperate girls in dire straits beg two minutes on the Ameche. Have a heart!* She sent it over with the waiter, but the man at the corner table didn't even glance up.

"I hope he goes to jail," Melba said.

"Me, too."

We ordered more champagne and began to devour the rolls and breadsticks. "If Skinny doesn't pick up the check we're dead," Melba said. Skinny was the owner, and he was fat, of course.

"We can always charge it," I said. I thought it better not to mention the roll of bills she had in her purse.

Across the room there were two young couples, the men glancing furtively at us every once in a while. Melba began flirting with one.

"That one's mine," she said, "and the blond one's yours."

"I don't like the blond one."

"O.K. I'll trade you. I was only being nice. The blond one's cuter. They're married, you can tell."

"How can you tell?"

"They wouldn't be out with two such ugly chicks if they weren't their wives."

In the opposite corner was a television star with his wife and his agent and his business manager. "I want to meet *him*," Melba said.

"The actor?"

"No, his agent. I need an agent. I could do commercials. You don't have to act, they dub it. And you can make ten thousand dollars on a commercial."

"Not if you don't talk you can't."

"I know you can." She took a stack of unpaid bills out of her purse, a roll of stamps, a stack of envelopes and a checkbook, and began writing out checks. The television star's agent looked at her. I had met him once, and he recognized me. We smiled at each other, nodded, and looked the other way again. "You know him!" Melba said.

"Yes, kind of."

"You have to introduce me."

"When we're leaving, if he's still here," I said, with no intention of leaving until after they had gone.

The captain ushered two middle-aged men to a banquette table opposite us. One of them was a movie producer I had been introduced to at a cocktail party the previous winter, and the other one I had never seen before. I knew the producer lived in California and commuted a lot. Melba kept on writing out checks and putting them into envelopes, licking and sealing the flaps, stamping the envelopes, writing addresses on the envelopes that were not already printed. She had enormous bills for one month: forty-seven dollars to the cleaner, fifty-six to the drugstore, but only five dollars to the neighborhood grocery. The producer's friend started to look at her with amusement.

"What do you have to do that here for?" I said.

"Might as well do them while I have the money in the bank."

It was as if the resturant was her office. Then the captain came over with the telephone and plugged it into the wall for us and that made it look even worse.

"You can have it for only two minutes," he said, glancing at the vice king or whoever he was in the corner. "The gentleman reserved it for the whole evening."

"I hope he goes to jail," Melba said again.

"He's a very good customer," the captain said.

As soon as the captain walked away Melba took her address book out of her purse. "Who shall we call?"

"I thought you wanted to call somebody!"

She was looking through her book. "Let's see . . . he's out of town . . . he's probably in bed with some chick; well, let's try." She dialed a number and got the answering service, she left her name and the name of the resturant. She dialed two more men, but both of them were out. Five minutes had passed, but the captain seemed to have forgotten us.

"I hate to see a good phone go to waste," Melba said. "I'll call my girlfriend in California."

"They'll get it on the bill!"

"Shh . . . cool it. I'll use the area code." She dialed the number in California and got her girlfriend's answering service. "Just tell her Miss Melba Toast called," Melba whispered, "from New York. Thank you, dear."

Both the producer's friend and the producer were now looking at us with amusement mixed with curiosity. The vice king was trying to summon the waiter and looking very displeased.

"Let's call Lem," Melba said. "He's on a business trip to San Francisco. I have the number."

"I don't like Lem."

"Just to say hello," she said. She dialed the number in San Francisco with the area code, and when the hotel operator told her Star Sapphire was out, she left both our names. That made me angry.

"He's going to think I like him," I said, "and I don't like him."

"Why are you so boring tonight?"

The captain came over and unplugged the phone, explaining that one had to be fair and share, and we were being unfair, and the gentleman really needed to make some calls. Melba looked over at the gentleman and smiled thank-you. He glared at her.

"Boy," Melba said, "George Grouch over there."

"Well, he's going to jail, he's probably upset," I said.

"He won't go to jail," Melba said. "People like that always beat the rap."

The two young married couples paid their check and left the restaurant. On the way out the blond one turned and looked back longingly at Melba. We both smiled wickedly at him.

"Married," Melba said. "Poor guy."

"Their wives are lucky," I said.

"Lucky? Why? Those two guys are just itching to bust out. Don't you think they cheat whenever they can?"

"I doubt it. They're too young."

"Nobody's too young," Melba said. "Boy, it's dead in here. Let's find some action. I know a swinging place. I'm going to ask for the check, and you start praying."

The captain came over to say that we were Skinny's guests and there would be no check. Melba pretended to be surprised and thanked him happily. She left a dollar for the waiter and we started for the door. The Hollywood pair were leaving, too, stopping to talk to the television star's agent. When we got to where they were all standing by their table near the door, Melba pushed me and I stepped on the agent's foot.

"How are you?" he said.

"Fine, thank you. And you?" We shook hands, and then because Melba was standing there with a little-kid-at-Christmas look on her face, I introduced them.

"I think I met you in Hollywood," Melba said.

"It's possible."

"I made a few movies there. I'm in New York looking for a new agent."

"Melba Toast . . . I don't think I'd forget a name like that," the agent said.

"I changed it. You may have heard of me under my real name."

I hoped she would think of a good real name, because I was getting ready to pretend to faint so we could get out of there. But the producer's friend seemed perfectly happy with her present name.

"You fascinated me," he said. "I kept watching you

70

at that table, writing letters and talking on the phone."

"I met you at a cocktail party," I said to the producer.

"Oh, yes," he said vaguely. "I remember very well."

The agent introduced everybody. I told the television star I was a fan of his, and smiled a lot at his wife, who smiled gratefully at me, and Melba announced to nobody in particular that we had just been to a cocktail party.

"We just flew in from the Coast," the producer said. "I can't get used to the time. I can't get used to having dinner at one in the morning. We had dinner on the plane, too. I'm exhausted from eating."

"Your face looks very familiar," the producer's friend said to Melba. "I think I may have known you on the Coast."

"Everybody knows me on the Coast," Melba said.

I said good night and headed for the door, only this time there were four of us, not really together but not really separate either. "Where are you girls going?" the producer's friend said.

"Carol's," Melba said.

"Well, then you can take the first cab. We're going to the hotel."

When we got into our taxi Melba gave the driver the address of Carol's Club, then she smacked herself on the head. "They thought Carol was the name of one of our girlfriends! Of course—they're from out of town, how would they know? They wanted to go with us but then they thought we wanted to shake them. Oh shit, what are we going to do?"

The cab containing our two Hollywood catches was just alongside ours at the red light. I rolled down my window and waved at them. The producer's friend rolled down his window and looked out. "Come with us!" I shouted. He nodded. "Follow our cab!" He nodded again, happily, and leaned over to tell his driver.

"You didn't have to be so forward," Melba said to me.

Carol's Club is one of those small West Side places; it stays open almost all night because of some technicality that makes it a private club. It has music and red lights and good liquor, and terrible sandwiches that cost five dollars. Everybody there looks like he's from another world: the girls all in silver lamé at three A.M. of a working-day morning, the men jovial and rested, leaning on the piano, holding heavy cut-glass highballs—the same men who will be sitting at desks in only six hours.

Melba was greeted with hugs and shrieks of joy. She made the rounds in the crowded room, so when we finally got a tiny table against the wall we couldn't find her. Then she bobbed up from the crowd, borne to us on waves of friendship, and sat down next to the producer's friend and ordered champagne and a package of Russian cigarettes.

"What are we doing in a place like this?" the producer said.

"This is supposed to be a business trip," the producer's friend said. "I'm his Story Editor. We have to be up at eight in the morning for meetings."

"You don't know how to enjoy yourself," Melba told him. "It's your first night in New York—swing."

"We come to New York almost every month," the producer said. "However, this is a very nice place."

"You girls can sleep late," the Story Editor said.

"I can't," said Melba. "I'm up at eight o'clock for my singing lesson. And then I take my dance class. And in the afternoon I have my acting class."

"Where do you study acting?" the producer asked her.

"Oh, let's not talk shop." She held out her glass of champagne. "Taste this if you want to taste something good."

"Champagne gives me a headache," the producer said. "I have to sound bright tomorrow morning."

I began to like him. He was quiet and dignified and seemed totally unaware that Melba was about to pluck his feathers. He acted as if he had wandered by mistake into a kooky situation with two of his daughter's friends. He was very good-looking in an aristocratic way, which was unusual for a movie producer because most of them look like garment salesmen, which is what they were before they became artists. He had marvelous wrinkles when he smiled, the kind that make you think they say something. Not golf wrinkles, character wrinkles.

The other one, his Story Editor, looked more lively,

but he looked as if he was thinking of a way to make this unexpected hour of frivolity into a business deduction. I wished I could think of something intelligent to say to him so he would feel better.

Melba was sitting there, perfectly confident, sipping her champagne and smoking her thin black cigarette, a girl who had long since become accustomed to the fact that her mere presence constituted a business expense.

"One more drink and then we have to go to sleep," the Story Editor said.

"The night is young," Melba said.

"Well, I'm not," said the producer. I thought he was a man who would never cheat on his wife and I liked him. I began to feel as if I had to protect him from Melba and me, to keep him safe and good and guileless. I thought how nice it would be to be married to him. I knew I must be getting drunk.

When we left Carol's Club the piano player was still playing, the silver lamé girls and happy men were still hanging around the piano, and time in that rosy-lighted place was still stopped. It seemed as though if we returned there a year later the same people would still be there, still bright-faced and not a minute older.

"You girls drop us off at our hotel," the Story Editor said in the cab, "and then you go on to wherever you live." He gave some money to the driver. "This should get you there."

"But we haven't eaten dinner!" Melba shrieked.

"I can not eat another dinner tonight," the producer said. He looked amused and pained, just like a good father at three-thirty in the morning with two energetic daughters.

"Well then," Melba said, "at least give us some money to eat with."

I looked at the door next to me and wondered if I could dive out of it without getting killed. On the other hand, I thought, if I get killed I will feel better.

The Story Editor looked at the producer and then back at us. He reached into his pocket again. "Here's ten dollars," he said. "That ought to buy you both breakfast anywhere you want to go."

Oh, God, I thought, ten dollars—he still thinks we're nice girls. I looked at the door longingly and knew I would never have the courage, so I shrank into the corner behind the handle.

The cab drew up at their hotel, an elegant old hotel on Fifth Avenue, and the two men got out. Melba jumped out after them. She grabbed the producer by the hand.

"It was a pleasure meeting you," she said. "I'd love to see you again tomorrow night. Let's have dinner at—"

"Call us," the producer said, pulling his hand out of Melba's grip, and heading for the entrance to his hotel. He was running.

"I'll call you," the Story Editor squeaked, running too. They disappeared into their hotel. Melba got back into the cab.

"Well," she said, pleased, "we have a dinner date for tomorrow night."

I almost believed her. How wonderful, I thought, to have tomorrow all planned, and with such nice men. . . .

"How much did he give you?" Melba asked the driver.

"Two dollars."

"O.K., drive around for a minute." She looked at the ten-dollar bill in her hand and then turned to me. "Well," Melba said, "is it five apiece, or do we eat?"

I pictured a box of lovely five-dollar dusting powder in a white shiny plastic box with a fat lambs-wool puff, looking elegant on top of the radiator cover in my bathroom . . . and its party scent. I imagined a small bottle of Chanel cologne, slim and squarish and pristine and sexy. Things . . . trophies . . . anesthetics. . . . Life isn't a process of change, it's just a series of little decisions, so small, most of them, that you don't even notice when you're making them; only when you discover the kind of person you have become.

"We eat, of course," I said.

"We might as well," Melba said. "You can't do much with five dollars anyway."

She gave the driver the name of a French place that stays open twenty-four hours a day and was just around the block. We stopped in front of it and she said to the driver: "Listen, can you wait here for us until the deuce runs out?"

He laughed at her, so we got out and he drove away.

The place was too brightly lit for me after the darkness of the cab, and everybody looked sleepy. There was a conveyor belt with fresh fruit that looked too big and shiny to be real, and trays of enormous high cakes. I ordered a *Croque Monsieur* and a quarter liter of rosé, and Melba ordered scrambled eggs with sausages and a bagel with cream cheese and strawberry jam and hot chocolate, and then she didn't eat any of it. I ate mine and was halfway through hers when a drunk from another table came over and sat down beside me. He was about our age, a little older.

"Hello, girls."

"*Va t'en,*" I said.

"Do you girls speak English?"

"Not a word," Melba said coldly. "We come from South America. Beat it."

"You speak English," he said. "Let's be friends."

"Sir, will you kindly leave?" Melba said.

"Come on . . ." The drunken nastiness was just underneath his tourist friendliness, like a poisoned cupcake under pretty icing. "Talk to me."

Melba gestured for the manager.

"I just want to have a drink with you girls," the drunk said. He was neither handsome nor ugly, just ordinary and square and poor. Rich enough to get drunk in that place, but not rich enough to talk to Melba.

"All right, my friend," the manager said. He took the drunk by the arm and led him back to his table where he had been sitting with a woman and another couple.

"I'm sorry," the manager said to us. "Some nights we just can't keep them quiet. Seems like they always get friendly at this hour."

"Why can't people just leave other people alone?" Melba said.

"He's with his wife," the manager said. "I don't think he'll bother you again. I apologize."

"Two girls alone can't even eat in peace," Melba said.

The drunk stood up again and tried to leave his table, but this time a waitress and a busboy stopped him.

"I think his wife is drunk too," I said.

"I can't understand some people," said Melba. "Why don't they just go home where they belong?"

"Don't I wish it," the manager said.

When we finished dinner there was enough money left for cab fare for both of us. Melba wanted me to go home with her and stay over, but I knew she would play records all night and tell me about the men who were devotedly in love with her, and I was not up to it, so I dropped her off in a cab and went home to my own apartment and went to bed.

The last thing I thought when I fell asleep was how nice it was that we were going to have dinner with the producer and his friend. It was really something to look forward to.

But of course they never called, and we never saw them again. At least, I never did. I didn't hear from Melba that week, so I have no way of knowing if she called them at their hotel the next day when they didn't call us. In the morning I had forgotten both their names, but I knew she had remembered. And by the time I did talk to her again there was something else happening, and so I forgot to ask her what happened to that imaginary dinner date . . . and what had happened to those two tennis players, who might just have been real, and who had started the whole thing in the first place.

I was sitting under the dryer at the hairdresser's reading a gossip column when I read that Tigercat had eloped with some society girl. I knew what that would do to Melba and I was worried. It's one thing to be jilted by a professional bachelor and become one of the club, but when some other girl actually marries him there's a distinct sense of failure. Even Melba had to feel that. I know I always did. I wondered if she knew yet.

She called me that night. "I have to get away," she said. Her voice was calm, but too tight, and I knew she knew. "Come with me."

"Where?"

"I don't care . . . Nassau, Barbados, I have friends . . ."

"I can't go, I haven't any money. And the analyst

. . . And if I don't go to auditions I won't work all winter."

"You don't need money," Melba said. "I don't have any money either."

"Let me think about it."

"Well, I'm going," she said, and hung up.

I called her the next day but her service said she was out of town and they didn't know where.

I went through the motions of my life for the rest of the fall, hanging on, going through the motions of being well adjusted and getting well. I went to auditions for parts I did not get, I called about auditions I was not allowed to go to, I saw other people in my acting class with far less talent than I had getting good parts (or isn't that what we always think, that they have less talent than we do?). I went to the doctor, I took my nice sleeping pills, I smoked too much, and I hated everybody. From time to time, when I was out, my service received a phone call from Melba, long distance, but I knew there was no hope of finding her because the number the operator left was always a hotel or a restaurant where she had alighted for a few hours, where someone was paying the phone bill. I wanted to find her because I wanted to join her. Even without money and without friends she was alive, she was somewhere, and I was half dead and nowhere.

One evening I had some friends over for dinner, and when we were just sitting down to eat Melba finally called. She was in Hawaii.

"I've been trying to get you for months," she said. "You have to pack up right now and join me. All I do is go to Watusi parties and go surfing, and you'll never guess who I'm staying with."

It was a movie star, of course. He had rented a home there. I remembered him from the movie magazines as a handsome, eligible young bachelor, and from New York gossip as fat, sloppy, and a fag. But still, I was jealous, because I knew that if I had gone to Hawaii I would never have met him at all, and Melba was living with him.

"He's out working," she said. "I'm just lying here in bed calling all my friends. Listen, have you got a pencil? My service said these people have been calling me constantly, so I want you to call them for me, and don't tell them who I'm with; just say I'm in Hawaii for a rest. And if you want any of them, take them, because you might dig them."

"How am I supposed to get them?"

"You're smart, you'll think of a way. I don't have to tell you *everything*, do I?"

I wrote down their numbers, although I knew I would never call.

"All I do is drive around in Caddies and Porsches," Melba said happily. "And he's going to trade in his Caddy convertible for the new model. If I can find my own apartment for a bill and a half a month I may stay here for a year. I'm going to buy a little motorcycle to get around on."

I could just see her, in her bikini, driving a red

motorcycle. I didn't even have the courage to be a passenger on one. I didn't have the courage to do anything.

"Tell me about him," I said.

"Well, he's kind of immature, that's his only fault, but he's intelligent. He wants to be a writer. I'm helping him write a story. You should see this house. From where I'm lying in bed all I can see are palm trees and frangipani and passion flowers; miles of trees and flowers. It's like paradise."

"He's fat," I said.

"But he's trying. What I mean about immature, well, he has this food fetish, and he keeps all the cookies and crackers and peanut butter locked in a safe in the kitchen, and nobody knows the combination but his secretary and the houseboy and me. Sometimes in the middle of the night he makes me work the combination, and then he sits in bed in front of the TV set gobbling. There are always food stains on the sheets. But he's trying, and we have fun together."

"He's gay," I said.

"He is not!"

"Well, I'll take your word for it."

"I can give you my solemn word he is not gay. Listen, don't tell anybody in New York about us, don't even mention his name, because I don't want to lose all my men. I might come back, you know."

"All right," I said, "I won't mention his name."

"Seriously," Melba said, "why don't you come

down and visit us? Donald Dirtysheets is dying to meet you, I told him all about you."

"Maybe he has a nice friend," I said. "Who only drinks."

"He has millions of friends. This place is loaded with groovy bachelors, much better than New York. The handsomest men I ever saw. New York is *nowhere*. You've got to come to Hawaii."

"How did you get to meet him in the first place?"

"Well, you know I wanted to get away. So I took a plane to Seattle, because there was this man I dated who lives there and I thought I'd surprise him, but when I got there he told me he was leaving the next day for New York. He insisted on paying me back for my plane ticket, though. He went to New York and left me sitting there in the hotel, so I had a fast one-minute cry and then I said to myself, Don't be a fool. So I called a guy I used to go with in California, and his secretary said he had gone to Honolulu, so I took a plane to Honolulu. He was very nice; he said to cheer up, and he took me to a party. There I met some other people who invited me to another party, and at the other party I met Donald Dirtysheets. He dug me right away, so we began seeing each other, and when he saw the roach hole I was living in he insisted I pack up everything and move into his house. We said it would be just temporary, but I'm still here. You wouldn't know me—I have a tan, I'm a platinum blonde, and I look so healthy."

"With a frangipani blossom over one ear."

"The health stuff," Melba said. "There's nothing like it. Life *au naturel*. Bikinis all day and slacks at night. Dancing and surfing."

"Peanut butter in bed."

"Guess who I just called," she said. "Tigercat! I phoned him to congratulate him on his marriage, and we agreed to remain friends. You see, I'm over him."

"What did he say about your being in Hawaii with a movie star?"

"Oh, I didn't tell him. I called him at his office and he was in the middle of a conference, so we could only talk for two minutes. You've *got* to come to Hawaii and dig the available men. You're a fool if you don't fly down."

My guests began to scream at me that the spaghetti was getting cold, so I told her I would have to get off the phone. She didn't want to let me go, but finally, after I took the private number and promised to call the following week, we said goodbye. I wondered what Donald Dirtysheets would say when he got his phone bill.

"What's the matter?" my guests said. "Why are you so depressed? How do you know she's telling the truth? You believe everything."

That's what I told myself, too . . . and I remembered that my analyst had suggested that someday Melba would find a few wrinkles and then what would she have; but I wondered what did I have now?

Did any of them really love her? Did it matter, since Melba believed they did, then and afterward? Not to believe it she could not have survived. How many of us, loved after someone's fashion, never quite believe it, or believe it but wish it was more?

She did not have the good things in life, if good things are a home and children and someone who comes back to be there with you. But she had many homes, all of them impossibly glamorous, and she had many children, all of them the men she taught to revere her, and she always had someone who came back to be with her and take her to the places she thought were the big world.

The Someones changed, but does not even one special someone change through the years, from eagerness to dissatisfaction to—hopefully—mellowness and a new kind of love? Melba had all that in microcosm. She had all that and more. She had first love and sorrow, she had power and humiliation, she had lies and the deepest kind of frightening truth. For she saw into the secret places of men's dreams, the dreams that made them forever mortal and forever vulnerable; and so, was she not in a way a banker of something far more precious than money?

She *knew* . . . and she knew what most women only suspect. For most women are lucky; they see their love turn mortal, they grow old and sad and weary, and then finally peaceful and smug. But Melba always saw, over and over, and so she knew that at the end there is no unique mystery, but only

the pathos and ugliness and sweetness of people trying to like each other, trying to feel something, trying to laugh and be gay to hide their failure. And
nevertheless, she survives.

I knew I had to make a decision about my own
life. I could hock something and fly to Hawaii to stay
with her, provided her host would really be so glad
to see me, or I could stay here and forget it, or . . .
I could stay here and try something new. I knew her
so well by now that I knew everything she did and
how she did it. Oh yes, I was her pupil all right, the
inheritor of her survival kit. It was just a matter of
emotional fortitude, persistence, and a little hard-
hearted technique.

It embarrasses me to tell what followed, but it's
important, so I'll tell it. I picked out a man at a party
—divorced, fairly successful, not old, not too ugly—I
liked him, he liked me, so I went to dinner with him
at an in restaurant, ate nothing, ordered a great deal
of champagne, and at two in the morning I made
him stop off at an all-night drugstore to buy me a
toothbrush and I went home with him and stayed for
four days.

It is easy to stay at a man's apartment for four days:
you just don't leave. It's always time for another meal,
or to make love, or you get involved in a long talk, or
you're asleep and he has to go to the office and doesn't
want to wake you. And then, when he comes back
from the office, there you are. You're not allowed to
answer his phone because it might be another girl, or

his mother; so he can't get any of his phone calls from those other girls and he has nobody to go out with and there you are. Of course you do answer his phone, and you tell the other girls *and* his mother that you're his new girl, and then you don't give him their messages.

While he's out you clean his apartment so he'll like you, and you wash your underwear, and you put on his bathrobe and call the three-hour cleaner down the street to pick up your cocktail dress and have it back before five o'clock. You also call the local drugstore for whatever cosmetics you need, and everything's cool. You never go home to change clothes until you're firmly entrenched—say a couple of weeks. If he's tired of what you're wearing he can take you out shopping.

Then, finally, the day comes when you really have to go home for something, or out for something— maybe a job you can't turn down, or the analyst— and there's where I made my first mistake. You never leave until you have a key. Even if you borrow the key to go downstairs to the grocery and have a copy made at the hardware store on the way back, you never leave without some key of his. You see, once you have his key, he either has to have a screaming fight with you or change the lock, and most men are too lazy to change the lock. A screaming fight is something you can sail through if you're a Melba.

But I think I made more mistakes than that, because they were creeping up on me, those mistakes.

Like, you do *not* accept a job, and you do *not* go to an analyst. You never give him any excuse to think you are either financially independent or neurotic. But you talk about how you love your career and how difficult it is to get anywhere.

So I left without a key and he said he would call me, and I waited for him to call. Mistake number ten. You *never* wait for him to call you; you tell him you don't know exactly where you'll be and you'll call him. Then you keep calling every ten minutes until you get him. There's no gambling that way. Social graces are dead, shyness is dead, chivalry is dead, tact is dead, game playing is dead, necking is dead, Mr. Right is dead, manners are dead, prudence is dead, expectations of any kind are dead. Only the moment lives. The moment is not an investment, it is an entity.

I sat out the first week like a catatonic, and the second week in a growing agony of paranoia. Then I started calling him, every night. He was never in. I thought hopefully that maybe he had been in an accident, but then I remembered Melba's lessons of courage, and at the end of the third week I finally caught him on the phone.

He seemed surprised and glad to hear from me. "I was just thinking about you, coming up in the elevator," he said. "I remembered I hadn't spoken to you for a long time and I was going to call you."

"What a coincidence."

"Yes," he said, "but then I didn't call you."

Little trill of laughter. "Why not?" Mistake—
never ask him to express his feelings; he might find
out what they are.

"I'm afraid of you," he said.

"Why in the world should you be afraid of me?"

"Well . . . oh, all right, I'll tell you. Because there's
a great need for love in you, and I can't give it. You
seem to be trying to connect with someone."

"You mean you?"

"Not just me. . . . I have the feeling you want a
relationship with everyone you go out with. You
want him to have emotions about you. Maybe this
is hurting you, what I'm saying, but I believe in
honesty. Without honesty there's nothing."

"Oh, yes," I said. "I believe in honesty, too."

All these rotten rats have one good quality they
like to feature whenever they have a serious talk:
with this one it was his honesty.

"And I'm afraid of that need in you," he went on.
"You're too vulnerable. Maybe you'll never find a
man who can give you all the love and security you
need. Maybe there's just too much of a void in you
ever to be filled."

What did I say in those long talks?

"On the other hand," he said, "maybe it's my de-
ficiency. Maybe I'll never be able to *give* to another
human being. I'm afraid I won't. I'm just too hostile
and locked-in. So you scare me."

"Well," I said, "would you prefer a grasping
nymphomaniac?"

"I hate grasping nymphomaniacs!" he said virtuously. "I want some sort of communication, some liking, or there's nothing."

"But not too much liking . . ."

"I never go with one girl for long," he said.

"You have to take your choice: she likes or she doesn't like. You can't measure it out. A girl in your bed who doesn't care for you is a slut, and a girl in your bed who does care for you is a threat. Right?"

"I guess that's true," he said. "Maybe it's all my fault. Oh, I'll call you again sometime. I'd like to have a drink with you. I'll call you soon. But I just wanted to be honest with you."

"Thank you," I said. "And I'll call you, too, sometime."

"Please do," he said. "I mean that."

I tore his telephone number into tiny pieces and burned them in the ashtray. Then I went to sleep without any sleeping pill and slept beautifully. I don't know why I slept so well, when I hated him so much.

Perhaps it was just because any decision at all is better than extended nothing.

Melba, why can't I be like you? I can't, that's all. Nobody can be like anybody. I did all the wrong things with that man, but it wouldn't have mattered either way, because I unerringly chose the wrong man to do them with. Melba would have known better: she wouldn't have picked him. And Melba doesn't even know what she's doing—if she did, she wouldn't be able to do it so well.

She's still in Hawaii with her movie star, and I'm still here, but a few things have changed. I've learned not to trust words any more. "No one can ever love me enough" means something entirely different depending on who says it, and who to, and therefore it doesn't mean anything at all. Maybe even "love" doesn't mean anything at all, since 99 per cent of the people who rely on the word have different ideas of its meaning. That sounds a little like a form of Zen; maybe I am getting to be more like Melba than I thought. . . .

No, no, no, no, no. You have to *be* Melba in order to be like her. Don't you?

Guess Who This Is

RICHARD VIKING AND CARLEN ADAMS, brilliant inventions of the new Hollywood—you can see them on the screen whether you want to or not. If you are invited, you can see them at Hollywood parties—conspicuously young and uncomfortable among the middle-aged producers, directors and vanishing core of middle-aged stars. The young couple do not look out of place in their dinner clothes; they look as if they were on their way to the college prom. It is possible to look both superior and shy at the same time. They do. They talk to no one. Several people speak to them; the producers and directors make a point of stopping to say a few polite words to them and then move on.

Carlen and Dick know the names of most of these

old people in the room, but not the names of their pictures. They have heard of Garbo (they once saw her in an art movie) and they put Gable in the same class with Hemingway: both are dead.

They are not child stars, as Mickey Rooney and Judy Garland were; they are adult stars. They do as they please. They make $200,000 apiece for one picture. They receive 10,000 fan letters a week. Before his recent marriage, a teen-age magazine ran a nation-wide essay contest: WHY I WOULD LIKE TO HAVE A DATE WITH RICHARD VIKING. It drew 175,000 entries in indifferent penmanship, some enclosing snapshots.

In the reviews of their motion pictures no one has ever mentioned their acting, either to criticize or to praise it.

They live in a mansion built by a star they think they once heard of. But the guided bus tours that show visitors a distant vista of stars' homes still say "This was once the home of Marlene Dietrich," not "This is the home of Carlen Adams and Richard Viking." After all, very few teen-agers have the patience for guided tours.

◄ᢒ

THIS October night the mansion at the top of Bene-dict Canyon looked like the *Queen Mary* at sea: hundreds of windows, all lighted, and everything around it black and still. It was a view never offered by the daytime tours. In the driveway, faintly illuminated from the picture window, were two small white sports cars with silver initials set into the doors: one marked HIS, the other marked ITS.

Richard Viking, the man of this house, wandered into the kitchen and searched around for the light switch. He was twenty-four years old, a little under six feet tall, with a handsome innocuous face. He was wearing long-sleeved flannel pajamas striped black and white to simulate a prison uniform, and he was barefoot. Around his neck under the pajamas he wore a thin gold chain bearing his wedding ring.

He found an opened box of chocolate-flavored breakfast cereal and poured some into a soup bowl, tapping his cigarette ash onto the floor. He poured milk over the cereal, but from the first whiff he could tell the milk was sour, so he left the bowl with its contents on the drainboard and looked through the refrigerator again until he found a can of butter-scotch-flavored Metrecal which he poured into a beer stein and took with him into the den.

The den was a long mahogany-paneled room with no furniture. There was a bar built along one wall and curving around the corner of the room, perhaps fifteen feet long in all, and he set the beer stein of Metrecal on this while he searched for cigarettes. The only decorations in the den were half a dozen eight-by-ten studio head shots of Richard Viking, in silver frames, and half a dozen similar photographs of Carlen Adams. The pictures of Richard were inscribed "To Carlen, with all my love," and the pictures of Carlen were inscribed "To Dick, with love forever." They were enlargements of the same photographs which Dick and Carlen sent to their fan clubs all over the country.

With two packs of cigarettes in one hand and the stein in the other, Dick left the den and walked through the living room on his way to the bedroom, which was at the opposite end of the house. The living room was enormous and empty. It was carpeted from wall to wall with thick pale-gold broadloom, spotlessly clean. The only furniture in the room was a large, pale-gold crescent-shaped couch, and against the opposite wall a color television-stereophonic hi-fi console, which had been given to him as a present from the producer of his last picture. Above the console was a framed oil painting of Carlen standing on a hill with her hair blowing in the wind, wearing an evening gown and holding her poodle.

Carlen was lying on the bed. She was wearing black-and-white striped prison pajamas to match her husband's, and without makeup she looked fourteen years old. She was actually twenty. She was a tiny girl with a pale, freckled, snub-nosed, frightened little face.

"How do you feel, honey?" he asked.

"Lousy. What have you got there?"

"There's nothing to eat in this house," he said. "For Crissakes, the milk is sour, there's nothing." He propped up his pillows and lay on the bed beside her.

"I'm sorry, honey, I forgot to go to the store."

"You're not supposed to *go* to the store, you're supposed to *call* the store," he said.

"I forgot." She started to giggle and then he laughed and hit her with the pillow.

"Stop it. I'm sick."

"I forgot," he said.

She hit him with the pillow for that, and he began to tickle her until she screamed and then he stopped.

"I'm bored," she said. "Let's call Gretchen."

"You call her."

She reached out lazily and dialed a number on the telephone that was on a cluttered table next to the bed. The entire bedroom was cluttered; in fact, it was the only room of the house that appeared to be lived in. It was furnished in seventeenth-century Spanish modern, and every available surface was covered with toys, dolls, teddy bears, framed photographs of Carlen and Dick, filled ashtrays, magazines, perfume bottles, ornaments, cosmetics and souvenirs. The bathroom, seen through the open door, looked like a department store makeup department. The closed toilet seat was covered with a ruffled black lace cover which their best friend, Gretchen, referred to as their "Mr. John hat."

Gretchen's voice, amplified and lifelike, came through a loudspeaker set into the wall above the bed. "Hello?"

"This is the Forest Lawn Cemetery," Dick said in sepulchral tones. "Is this Miss Gretchen Tennieson?"

"Yes . . . ?"

"I understand you have a pickup for us."

"You must have the wrong number."

"Is this Gretchen Tennieson?"

"Yes . . ."

"Well, you just go out in the garage and take a look. That's where it's supposed to be."

"Carlen!" Gretchen's voice shrieked. "Is that Dick?"

"Yes, it's us," Carlen said.

"Who's dubbing your pictures lately, Richard?"

"Ha ha," Dick said. "I had you fooled."

"Sure you did. What are you kids doing?"

"Carlen's sick."

"Are you sick, Carlen?"

"I'm all right, I just have a headache."

"Why don't you come over?" Dick said.

"I can't. I have a date."

"Is he there now?"

"Yeah."

"You both come over," Carlen said.

"You're sick," said Gretchen.

"I'm not that sick."

"We have to go out and eat," Gretchen said.

"Well, get some hamburgers or something and come over here," Dick said.

"He wants to go out."

"Oh, come on," said Carlen. "Don't be a pig. Come on over."

"I can't. I'll talk to you tomorrow."

"Oooh-oooh." Dick began grunting, moaning and

making obscene noises. "Gretchen wants to be alone. Who is he, Gretch?"

"You go to hell," Gretchen said. "Get well soon, Carlen." She hung up.

Dick and Carlen looked at each other and shrugged.

"What do you want to do?" Dick asked.

Carlen sighed. She tore open the pack and lit a cigarette. "You want to play with the phone?"

"You want to?"

She brightened. "Yah."

He reached to the table on his side of the bed and took the phone book. He lit a cigarette, put an ash-tray between them, and lay back, the opened telephone book on his stomach. "Me first?"

"Yah."

Dick closed his eyes and inscribed a circle in the air with his index finger. "Mmm . . . round and round it goes, and where it stops no-o-obody knows. . . . Krowkalski, H. G."

"What's the number?"

She dialed the number he gave her and they both listened, tensed and wide-eyed, as the loudspeaker on the wall sent forth the sound of the telephone ringing at the residence of Krowkalski, H. G.

"Yeah, hello." The man's voice was tired and slightly accented.

"Is this Mr. Krowkalski?" Dick said.

"Yeah. Who's this?"

"Tell me, Mr. Krowkalski, do you go to the movies?"

"Yeah, sure. What's this, a poll?" Krowkalski sounded bored. Carlen put her hands over her mouth to suppress a giggle.

"Not exactly. Who is your favorite young actor, Mr. Krowkalski?"

"Huh?"

"Your favorite young actor. Your favorite star. For example . . . do you like Richard Viking?"

"Yeah, he's all right."

"Have you seen his last two pictures?"

"Listen," Krowkalski said, the voice sounding more tired, "I got things to do. What's this about?"

"How would you like . . ." Dick said dramatically, "how would you like to actually *talk* to Richard Viking on the telephone?"

"What for?"

"Hang up," Dick said to Carlen. She did.

"I bet he's a plumber," Carlen said. She lit another cigarette. "He's watching TV. Krowkalski the plumber. Let me try one now."

"No, I want to do another."

"It's my turn. Come on . . . I'll do it for you, O.K.?"

"Oh, all right." Dick flipped over a handful of pages. He closed his eyes and his pointed finger circled, hovered, swooped down. "Waterford, Mae."

"Whee . . . that sounds like a good one." Carlen dialed, her eyes round and bright. The loudspeaker emitted the sound of four rings.

"The television set is far away from the telephone,"

Dick said. "Hurry up, Mae; 'Queen for a Day' is calling."

"Shhh!"

"Hello." The woman's voice was soprano and bright.

"Good evening, Mrs. Waterford," Carlen said sweetly.

"*Miss* Waterford. Yes?"

"Miss Waterford, do you go to the movies?"

"In this town? What a question."

"Oh, then you must have seen all the latest pictures."

"Who is this?"

"I'd just like to ask you a few questions, if I may," Carlen said.

"I'm used to questions," Miss Waterford said gaily.

"Well . . . do you like Richard Viking?"

"Richard Viking. . . . He's one of those young kids, isn't he?"

"He's the biggest new young male star."

"Star!" Mae Waterford said with contempt. "All those no-face kids are alike to me; I can't tell one from the other. Oh, yeah, he's the one married to that Carolyn what's-her-name, I remember. *Star!* I'll tell you a *star.* John Garfield, that was a star. He had a face, at least; you knew who he was. I may have been only a character woman, but a lot of people knew *my* face if they didn't know my name, and I worked with some *real* stars, and I can tell you—"

Carlen hung up.

"Boy!" Dick said. "Whew!" He turned up the collar of his pajamas and shuddered.

"Did you ever hear of her?" Carlen asked. "I didn't."

"Old bitch. John Garfield . . ." he mimicked in a falsetto voice. "I'll tell you a *star*. That Carolyn what's-her-name . . . let's try another number, *Carolyn*."

Carlen hit him on the side of the head with her clenched fist.

"Hey! You'll ruin the profile."

"You haven't got one," she said.

"Yeah, I forgot. No face. Shall we find another peasant to give a thrill?"

"Your turn."

"We'll try a nice, solid American family. Mmm . . . MacBrosnan, Robert L."

Carlen dialed the number and the two of them straightened up against their pillows. After a moment a young-girl voice answered.

"Mrs. MacBrosnan?" Dick said.

"No, it's Janie. Who's this?"

"Miss Janie MacBrosnan?"

"Yes . . ."

Dick winked at Carlen. "Tell me, Janie . . . do you like to go to the movies?"

"Sure."

"And do you have a favorite male star?"

"Uh huh."

"Who is it?"

"Well . . . Paul Newman. Um . . . do you want two?"

"Go right ahead."

"Well . . ." There was an exhaling of breath. "I just love Richard Viking."

The cigarette she was holding burned Carlen's fingers and she dropped it on the sheet with a shower of sparks. She was still slapping them out when Dick went on.

"Janie, how would you like to actually *speak* to Richard Viking? On the telephone."

The girl giggled. "Huh?"

"I mean it," he said.

"I'd love to," she said shyly.

"Well, Janie . . ." Dick said, "suppose this was Richard Viking talking to you right now . . . !"

"Huh?"

"Isn't my voice familiar?"

"I—don't know."

"You said you just love Richard Viking. Well, this *is* Richard Viking."

There was a silence. "Oh, sure," she said finally.

"It *is*."

"Really? The real Richard Viking?"

"Of course."

"Well . . . how come?" the girl asked, and giggled again.

"I can see you still don't believe me. All right, do you know who Richard Viking's wife is?"

"Sure. Carlen Adams."

"Is Carlen Adams also one of your favorite movie stars?"

"Sure."

Dick prodded Carlen on the leg with his bare toe. He nodded at her and pointed to the phone.

"Hello, Janie," Carlen said softly.

"Hello . . . ?" The voice from the loudspeaker was hushed, awed.

"Janie"—Carlen said, and now her voice was sure, louder, warm with generosity—"*Guess who this is!*"

He Can't Be Dead, He Spoke to Me

WE ARE distressed to learn that the sound of a human voice and the warmth of a human body can now be replaced by a machine. Called the Mother Machine, it is used in some nurseries; but adults need not feel left out, for soon science will find a machine companion for them. In the meantime there is a readily available substitute, which goes by the brand name of the Acquaintance, the Date, and sometimes (although the Better Business Bureau may eventually prosecute) the Friend. This product needs very little care, only occasional feeding, and is self-powered. When it starts to run down it can be plugged into any outlet in a lonely room for a week or ten days and it will be as good as new. Information on where to obtain the Acquaintance, the Date, or the Friend may be obtained by writing to . . .

✑§

IT WAS half past ten when the three of them finally made it to the restaurant in the Village, just before the kitchen closed. She was a rich girl who looked like a dancer, he was a vice president of a small advertising agency who looked like a vice president of a large advertising agency, and her friend was an actress who looked like a silent-movie star. They liked the way they looked. He was slightly drunk; the two girls were sober. For that reason, the girls were still boisterous and giggly, and he was being careful and precise. After four drinks he moved the hands as if he were smoothing a skirt. Her friend thought he was queer, but she knew he was not; it was just that he did not like anyone—not men, not women, not children, not animals. He liked bourbon and martinis.

She and her friend ordered complete dinners, he ordered a drink and a bottle of wine. He was on a diet and had lost ten pounds, but he had ten more to go. She had known him for two years, and she had known the actress six months, but she knew the actress.

It was Saturday night, which was of no importance to any of them. But to others in the resturant it was very important. The restaurant was a long, narrow room with a bar at the front and tables in the back, the two parts separated by a coat rack and a partial wall on which hung an open pay phone. The three of them were the only diners, but the bar was full.

"We're going to meet my friend here at eleven," he said. "When you meet the girl he's going with, don't be shocked."

"Why should we be shocked?" she said.

"You'll see. She has this talent for millionaires. One millionaire, she only has to take a walk around the reservoir with him every Wednesday afternoon and he gives her seven hundred dollars a week. She doesn't do anything else with him. No sex."

"A reservoir freak," she said.

"Oh, my God, I'm so hungry," the actress said. "I'm so hungry; oh God, hurry, hurry."

"I'm starving," she said. "I didn't eat all day. Waiter, please, bring some bread and water right now."

The waiter, who was young and looked like an unemployed folk singer, smiled at all of them and brought a basket of fresh Italian bread and three pats of butter on three small squares of paper.

"No class," she said. "When they're cheap with the butter you can always tell."

"You can have my butter," he said. "I don't need butter or bread or food. I stick to booze. Liquor isn't fattening."

"It is so fattening," the actress said. "It's more fattening than anything. Ask anybody."

"The martini is a killer," she said.

"Who says so?"

"Ann Landers. Dorothy Kilgallen. Dr. Rose Haus-frau. Paul V. Paul."

"Who's Paul V. Paul?" he said.

"My dermatologist."

The smiling waiter (who was smiling because he would be going home soon to his lovely young bride of eight months, whom he would catch with a Greek bartender, whom he would shoot at with his grand-father's dueling pistol and miss) brought two plates of beef stroganoff with noodles, a bottle of California red wine, and a martini.

One of the men had left the bar and was using the pay phone. They could hear him without difficulty so they listened, pretending not to.

"Hello," he said. "Hello? *Christ!*"

The actress laughed. Coins fell musically as the man slammed down the receiver.

The man ran his hand through his brush cut. "You say hello," he shouted, "and they disappear."

The actress laughed again, a little hysterically. "That's the story of my life," she said. "You say hello and they disappear."

She laughed too, and then he laughed because they were laughing, but the man at the wall, who was very much alone, put more coins into the telephone.

"Operator, I was talking to Millbank, New Jersey, and I was cut off. They did not hang up, you cut me off. You did. Well, try again."

"Oh, poor thing," she said. "Don't laugh, I can't hear him."

"Hello? Is Sally there? Oh . . . Jim, I'm sorry I woke you up. No, that's all right, I guess she'll call me tomorrow. . . ." His voice trailed off dispiritedly; he hung up and went back to the bar.

An older man who had been waiting took over the pay phone. He was wearing his overcoat and he had a German accent.

"Darling, what do you mean you can't go out? But *I* will give you your English lesson. I'll come over . . . oh. Well . . . then I suppose I'll see you sometime next week. It's just that last night was Friday, and I always see you on Friday night, so I wondered. . . . Well, perhaps next Friday then. Good luck with your English lesson."

"*Ich bin von Kopf bis Fuss* . . ." the actress sang.

"I am from—someplace," she said.

"No. 'I am from head to toe'—the way I am. Marlene Dietrich. *The Blue Angel.*"

"I thought Kopisfus was a town."

"No, Berlin is a town."

"I like it this way better. She's the way she is, and then she ruins that poor old man, right?"

"Right."

The man with the German accent and the overcoat went back to the bar. "Wouldn't it be funny if they were both calling the same girl?" the actress said.

"It's just that she has a German boyfriend," she explained, "and he's older."

"Sweetness!" the actress cried.

"When I was a little kid in school," the advertising man said, "I wrote this girl a love note. I still remember it. I wrote: 'I love you Geraldine. Do you love me? If you don't love me, pass this on to Harriet.'" He laughed. "*Pass this on to Harriet.*"

"Why did you write that?"

"I don't know. I wanted to make Geraldine jealous, I guess."

"Imagine Harriet getting that note."

"Well, I never really thought about that part of it."

"I love it," she said. "I love it, I love that note. *I love you Geraldine. If you don't love me, pass this on to Harriet.*"

"That's not what I said. I said . . ."

"It doesn't matter what you said. I love it. It's the story of my life."

"Oh? Which one are you?"

"I haven't decided yet. It's just the sentiment I love. The *relating*."

"I think it's funny," he said.

"I think it's funny. I think it's marvelous. I'm going to write it down." She took a pen from her purse and began to scribble on the edge of the mimeographed menu.

"Be sure you get it right this time," he said. "'I love you Geraldine. *Do you love me?*' Oh, here they are." He waved at two couples who had entered the room.

There were greetings, introductions, and furniture moving. The two girls were mermaids: waist-long straight hair, supple bodies, pretty faces, no makeup. One was a brunette mermaid and the other was a blonde mermaid. They wore cotton blouses and tweed skirts. One man was American and the other was English, and both were dead.

"I see you've eaten dinner," the blonde mermaid said.

"We didn't eat dinner," the dark mermaid said. "Only a pizza or something, I forget."

"You will have dinner, my little flower," the American said. "I will take you to the most glorious little place I know—later."

"Oh, all right," the dark mermaid said pleasantly, and smiled at her.

She folded the menu she had written on and put it into her purse. She looked carefully and long at the dark mermaid, wondering what it was she did with millionaires on walks around the reservoir that could be worth seven hundred dollars a week, and she noticed that the mermaid was looking carefully and long at the actress with complete absence of female rivalry but as if singling her out. The actress knocked the wine over, or maybe she had knocked the wine over. There was a spreading stain on the tablecloth and for a moment everyone pretended concern.

The waiter put a clean napkin over the wine puddle and they finished what was left in the bottle.

"Oh, my God," she said, "look what that girl's doing."

The brunette mermaid was sitting at the table naked from the waist up.

"She said her bra hurt," the American said. "She had to take it off right now."

The mermaid put the cotton blouse on again and buttoned it very slowly. Then she handed the brassiere around the table so they could all see what it looked like. It was one of those new ones that looked as if it had been made for a child; it was half undershirt and couldn't hurt anyone unless it was tied around her neck.

"Look at that bra," the American was saying. "Isn't it interesting?" The mermaid had not stopped looking at the actress's face all this time and was still smiling.

"Everyone thinks I'm a dike," the actress mumbled angrily. "Why does everyone always think that?"

"I like *my* bra," the blonde mermaid said. She had a sweet, soft voice. The blonde mermaid lifted her shirt briefly, revealing an enormous bosom and a black brassiere. The Englishman smiled, half proprietary, half proud.

She nudged her friend, who was still mumbling angrily about people thinking her a dike, and nodded toward the blonde mermaid. "Myrna Milk," she whispered.

"Nora Nursing."

"Theresa Tits."

"Wendy Willing."

"Ethel Eager."

"What are you two whispering about?" asked the adman, having found the last martini watery and signaling for the check.

"No one noticed," the Englishman chirped. "Did you see? No one at the bar even turned around."

"They never do," she said. They walked out a side door to the street, ladies preceding the gentlemen, and she was suddenly conscious of everything she was wearing under her wool dress—bikini pants (Elizabeth Arden, silk, nice), no stockings (leg makeup), no slip—aware of the contours of her body under the tight dress as they must look to the men, as if her individual contours were her new badge of identity. But she was not interested in these three men; she was interested in herself, as if she were both on a movie screen and in the audience, appraising the image and watching them look at it.

They walked ten blocks in the cold night air to an apartment house where there was supposed to be a party. But when they rang the buzzer downstairs two couples came out and waved them away.

"The party's over. Nobody there."

"The police came and broke it up."

"Why?"

"Too much noise. Who knows?"

"Let's go upstairs," she said. "I like policemen.

They're wholesome, fearless, brave, loyal and trusty. And good-looking."

"The cops are gone."

"Then let's go up," someone said.

"Nobody's there. You're too late."

They had acquired one of the couples, a cross-eyed young man with a build like Steve Reeves, and a thin blonde in a college-girl coat. He had a car.

"Can he see to drive?" the actress asked, and laughed.

They rode to the home of the dark mermaid: a high-ceilinged, cavernous apartment, shadowy, candle-lit, with great, dark reefs of antique furniture looming in corners, a shimmering white marble statue of a Grecian woman, live palm trees in pots, three balconies, a fireplace in each room, gleaming parquet floors, and a mink rug. The toilet was out of order.

A stereophonic sound system was hidden in a closet. Their hostess put on a twist record.

"Is there anything to drink?" the advertising man asked, but no one answered. The gestures of the hands were now more exquisite; he seemed to be tightrope-walking holding two teacups. "Look for something."

"In a strange house?"

"The kitchen, the kitchen."

"What do you expect from a mermaid?" the actress told him. "Give her a glass of water, she can live on it for a week."

The men removed the jackets. The brunette mermaid was doing the twist alone, gracefully, wearing nothing but the long white body, the tweed skirt, and black leather pumps. Standing, she was six feet tall. With the straight, dark hair reaching the waistband, this skirt looked wrong . . . it belonged on a Connecticut matron.

"Make yourselves comfortable," the American said.

"Do you want me to teach you the twist?" the dark mermaid asked her.

"Why not?"

"That's it. That's all there is to it."

"This is a beautiful apartment. Where did you get those wonderful antiques?"

"Oh, here and there."

The blonde mermaid wandered around for a while in a black lace brassiere, a skirt, a string of pearls, and long pearl earrings, and then went into the bedroom.

The Englishman and the American followed the blonde mermaid, the cross-eyed Hercules was looking for liquor, the advertising man had found a half-empty pint of vodka but no glass to put it in, the thin blonde had buttoned her college-girl coat up to the neck, the actress—who never smoked—was puffing nervously on a butt she had found in an ashtray, and she was inspecting the antiques.

She went into the bathroom, which was painted black, and looked through the medicine chest, finding mascara, skin food cream, glycerine soap, a Valentine card, a glass necklace (broken), cologne, a rusty razor blade, and seven currently active tooth-brushes. Next to the bathtub was a white telephone with an extra-long cord.

She went into the bedroom. It was dimly lit by candles on the window sills. The sky behind the candles was black; there were neither shades nor curtains. The furniture was strange and wonderful: a brass bed the size of the *Queen Mary*, an armoire that could hide three fully grown lovers or husbands, and an uprooted bidet planted full of pink flowers. There were two people in the bed and two people on the floor. At first she thought they were dead; then she saw that only the mermaids were. Indistinguish-able from one another in their whiteness, each couple, at first, seemed to be paired as it should be; then she realized that it was Be My Guest time. The dark mermaid was acceding limply to the Englishman, who was a foot shorter than she was, and her Ameri-can lover was lethargically asphyxiating the blonde, who still wore the necklace and earrings.

"Look what they're doing!" she said. "I've got to get my glasses."

When she returned wearing her glasses the two mermaids had begun to reveal that they were not dead after all, by making a few gracious noises. The others entered the room, one by one, stood around for a few moments, and went back to the music. The thin girl in the coat opened the front door quietly and slipped away.

The advertising man came back to the bedroom

and took her by the hand. "Come with me, I want to tell you something."

They went into the living room. "I don't like that," he said. "It doesn't entertain me. There's something . . . I don't know."

The actress and the cross-eyed boy whose vision she had doubted were kissing on the couch.

"Drink?"

"No, thanks. I wonder if she has 'Desafinado.'"

"I saw her put it on the machine."

"Oh, good."

"You don't want a drink?"

"Oh . . . all right. Aagh." She returned the bottle. "Warm vodka gives me heartburn."

"You're going *back* in there?"

"Just checking. Be right back."

When she entered the bedroom all four were now in the brass bed. They waved at her. "Come on in," they called cheerfully.

"No, thanks."

"Oh, come on. It's cold out there."

When she shook her head they went back to their new game. The blonde mermaid, who had not moved since they arrived, was being entertained by the two men and the other mermaid. The three were dividing the territory like a litter of newborn puppies, but not as eagerly.

The footboard of the giant bed made a not uncomfortable seat. She looked down at them, examining the sense of unreality she felt—the guilt, the curiosity, and above all, the boredom. *I'm a dirty voyeur,* she told herself, and waited for the thrill the words should evoke, but it did not come. *It's getting so I have nothing to tell my analyst any more.* . . . She found herself yawning. It was two o'clock in the morning. She could pick up the Sunday *Times* on the way home. . . .

"You're embarrassing me," the dark mermaid said, lifting the white, impassive face. "If you took off your clothes I'd feel better. You can still wear your glasses."

"Sorry. I won't watch any more."

"Oh, you can watch. But you look so *different* in that dress. If you were just like everybody else, we wouldn't notice you."

She climbed down from the footboard and went to the mirror to inspect her makeup. The advertising man returned, in his timid skin, preceded by the largest highball glass in the world, which he held like a fig leaf. "I didn't want to be a drag," he said apologetically. He sat quickly on a Louis XIV chair. "Come talk to me."

"How could you do a thing like that?"

"I'm sorry," he said. "Sheer oversight. I told you. You're not still mad? I *meant* to, but then I forgot to tell my secretary."

"I mean take your clothes off. Are you still harping on those theater tickets? I told you it didn't matter."

"Oh, the clothes. That's what you meant."

"Naturally."

He lowered his voice. "Confidentially . . . orgies make me impotent."

The group had completed their current game. The blonde mermaid remained supine. The pearls glimmered on the white throat. The shadowy eyes flickered toward the Englishman, who, as her date for the evening, had done most of the work. "That was nice," she said pleasantly.

"I don't know why you don't join us," the dark mermaid said. "We're all good friends."

"I prefer choice," she said, "and I wouldn't like to insult anyone."

"Oh, nobody would be insulted. I'm a good hostess, and believe me, nobody ever gets forced in my home. I mean, I would never invite anyone who tried to force himself on a guest. If you don't want me, I certainly wouldn't dream of forcing myself on you."

"It's too difficult to explain," she said.

The doorbell rang.

"Cops!" the adman cried. "Don't answer it!"

"Silly," the dark mermaid said, and went to the door. No one moved, except the adman with his highball glass, who was trying to decide between the armoire and the bathroom and crouched paralyzed between them.

The dark mermaid returned. "It's that other girl— the one who went home? She couldn't find her way, so I put her to sleep on the couch."

"Couldn't find her way home?"

"Well, she's drunk," the dark mermaid said kindly, and hopped back on the bed.

She went into the living room to look for her friend. But the actress and the cross-eyed boy had vanished. Then she noticed that a partition made of bits of furniture and a screen had been erected in a corner of the room. For the first time, she felt an emotion—loneliness.

The cross-eyed boy's girl, who had been dozing on the couch, sat up, looked around, saw the partition, and slammed out of the apartment again without a word.

"What was that?" the advertising man said, wandering back to find his bottle.

"That's the only girl who ever had a chance to walk out on her date twice in the same night."

"Talk to me." He sat on the couch behind the glass and bottle, like a giant newborn baby. She sat beside him in her wool dress. The actress emerged from behind the screen, partly clothed, neat and unruffled.

"We discussed it," the actress said, "and we decided against it." She sounded relieved.

"That poor guy," he whispered, gesturing toward the partition from which King Kong was emerging with a dazed look on his face. "Girls always go after him because he looks like such a stud. And all he wants is for *one* girl to want him for himself, not just use him."

"That's me," the actress said. "Everybody's mother."

The boy had decided he was in love with her.

"Look at me," he kept saying happily, "I got the prettiest girl at the party. Look at that! She's the best, the prettiest, the most wonderful girl in the whole room."

"Hello, mama," the actress said, and drank some of the vodka from the bottle.

"The prettiest girl in the whole place. Let's go out for breakfast."

"This is my year," the adman was saying. "I'm going to make it this year. Quit my job and write a book. My star is up. When my star is up, I know it. And this year my star is up." He was very drunk. "I mean, you understand—you have money and you know how it changes your life. And I'm going to have a lot of money this year. It's my year, and I'm going to be rich—as rich as you. Because my star is up."

The actress looked at him and fled into the bedroom, her hands over her mouth.

"Why don't you get dressed?" she said. "Everybody's going to go out for breakfast."

"Never eat breakfast. Let's go to my place and have a drink."

"I have to go to sleep. It's four-thirty."

He dressed, and the dark mermaid came into the living room and began putting sheets on the couch.

"You sleep out here?" she asked the mermaid.

"No. But somebody might."

The actress came back and put on her gloves. "Good night. Thank you very much."

"You're leaving already?"

They all shook hands—the four in their street

clothes and coats, the dark mermaid cool, white, lithe and charming. She was so much at ease that she seemed clothed. "It was nice meeting you. I hope I see you again."

"Hope so too. Thank you. Good night."

The blonde mermaid, who had not sat up for five hours, remained in the bedroom. The dark mermaid opened the front door.

None of them said anything on the way out. But when they reached the street they saw the velvet curtains part on the front window facing the street, and the flash of white bodies as their hostess and the American waved good night to them, smiling gaily. Then they all waved back, and laughed with relief to be free.

The two couples parted at the nearest all-night cafeteria. She got into a cab with her date, the young advertising executive whose star was up. For a while neither spoke. The cab rattled through the quiet Sunday morning streets. Finally he leaned toward her.

"I don't equivocate," he said. "Yes or no?"

"No," she said.

He drew back, injury and bewilderment on his face. "You *rejected* me!"

They rode the rest of the way to her apartment in silence.

Love Me, Love My Dog

D<small>R.</small> M<small>OLINARI</small>'s Licensed Massage Institute, Waxing, Pedicure and Consultations, is like hundreds of similar places in any American city where women go to be made perfect. It is perhaps less glamorous and more scientific than some, a little dirtier, but it has a reputation: models and actresses go there. One model walking out of a Dr. Molinari's is worth twenty civilians, an actress is worth from five to ten, depending on how old she is known to be and how young she looks. A series of massages, steam baths, or whatever, is called a Course, giving the passive body on the massage table the feeling that she is somehow learning something . . . like how to be a vegetarian, a yogi, or a better human being.

The place is presided over by six masseuses with

thick legs and orthopedic shoes. Dr. Molinari claims to be in his seventies, although he looks fifty; he eats secret salami sandwiches in the back room, and women clients are always trying to get the last appointment in the afternoon so they can be alone with him.

"Whew," he says in the morning, "I'm exhausted. That crazy woman, the blonde with the backaches, she insisted I take her out last night. She wouldn't let me alone. What do they chase me for? Hookers!"

Fur coats hang like moss on the clothes tree in the front hall; within is a row of tiny dressing rooms with cigarette butts littering the floors, then a row of massage tables separated by beaverboard partitions, and further within is the sanctuary. There, ladies lie on wooden beach chairs, their bodies encased to the waist in plastic space suits filled with hot, damp Epsom salts. The longer they sit there the more perfect their bodies will become, but their faces are from the Grand Guignol. They scowl, they frown, they stare at one another and avert their eyes, they smoke endlessly, they leaf through tattered movie magazines, and some of them talk.

The talkers fall into two categories: those who bring a friend, and those who think the masseuse is their analyst. The latter are found in the twilight areas between the beaverboard partitions, eyes shut, bodies in the Freudian position, free-associating nonstop in loud, clear voices. When the masseuse occasionally finds someone who does not like to speak during the hour, she can't quite adjust to it . . . she thinks the client does not like her, or that she has failed in some way. She asks, "How was your weekend?" even if it is Thursday.

The talker who brings a friend is found in the space-suit room. Sometimes both are taking a Course together, but often one is an outsider, perched on the end of the client's beach chair, looking overdressed, like a visitor to a sickroom.

On one rainy February morning there was a pair of these friends, Mona and Charlotte. Mona, the one in the space suit, was a model, she was mouse-colored and not particularly pretty without her makeup, but you could tell she was a model by the overstuffed tote bag and portfolio of photographs beside her chair. The visitor, Charlotte, wore a black dress and a great deal of gold-washed metal jewelry. The air was heavy with the scent of chain-smoked, filter-tip cigarettes. All the chairs were occupied.

"How's Bobbie?"

"Funny you should ask me that," Mona said. "I saw her last night. I hadn't seen her for about six months. She came over to say goodbye. She's getting married tomorrow."

"Oh, that's nice. Same guy?"

"Oh, no. Not that no-good rat. This one's a French photographer. They're going to live in Paris. She's flying there tonight to join him and then they'll get married there."

"How does she look?"

"Marvelous."

"I ought to run over there this afternoon and say goodbye," Charlotte said. "Maybe bring her a little present. I haven't seen her for so long."

They lit fresh cigarettes. The maid brought tea in paper cups.

"Bobbie says she's afraid to fly," Mona said. "But you know how she is—once she's in the air she'll love it. Silly how after flying all over the world and everything, modeling, she should still be scared of planes."

"She'll make a friend the minute she's on the plane," Charlotte said. "Bobbie always makes friends. They'll talk and eat and drink a little champagne—and before she knows it she'll be in Europe."

"Sure. That's what I told her."

"What ever happened to that other guy, though? The one she was going with? They must have gone together more than a year."

"The rat?"

"He was a rat?"

"Rat!" Mona said. "King of the rats. A little crazy even. And you know how he always seemed so sweet and well-adjusted? Like if they were watching television or something and Bobbie wanted ice cream, he'd run right downstairs to the drugstore and get it. He had at least ten pictures of Bobbie in his apartment—really, it was like a shrine. Who'd ever know he was a kook? I mean, he was in *advertising*."

"I always thought he looked like Robert Taylor," Charlotte said. "When he was young."

"When who was young?"

"Robert Taylor."

"Oh." Mona thought about it. "I thought he looked more like Tyrone Power."

"Same thing."

"I guess so."

"Well, anyway," Charlotte said, "what did he do that was so terrible? This rat."

"Alan, his name was. Alan."

"Alan Rat. What'd he do?"

"Well . . . step on that, will you? The butt. Thanks. Well, it was appalling. You'll think I made it up. I swear to God you'd have to have a devious, *warped* mind to make something like this up. What he did." Mona took another cigarette and lit it. "It was just so *planned*. If a man wants to break up with a girl, O.K., let him tell her, let them have it out. Or even if he runs away—there are rats like that—but at least it's *almost* normal. I mean, people do it. But this Alan . . . You know Hart? Bobbie's spitz dog?"

"That white dog? Sure."

"Well, you know, Hart is Bobbie's middle name. It's a family name. So when she got the spitz, she was so crazy about him she named him her own middle name. That's cute, isn't it?"

"My!" Charlotte said. "I never even knew that. I always thought it was *Heart* with an *e*. Like 'dear heart.'"

"Well, it was that too, I guess. I mean, Hart was

just like Bobbie's own heart and soul. He slept in her bed every night."

"How did Alan like that?" Charlotte asked.

"I guess they stayed over at his place if they wanted to do anything," Mona said, after some thought. "Because I remember Bobbie told me once that Alan always had to take her home after to walk the dog, and that boy used to get upset about it! He said some terrible things to her. Imagine . . . he told her it was understandable for a *man* to want to get up and go home after he'd been with a girl he wasn't in love with, but if a girl was in love with a man it was *unnatural* for her to want to get dressed and go home in the middle of the night. He thought he was Dr. Kinsey or something. Imagine telling his fiancée she was unnatural! I think he was just lazy. He used to say that Bobbie didn't really love him."

"I don't know why they couldn't just lock the dog in the bathroom," Charlotte said. "I mean, it doesn't take *that* long."

"Well, see," Mona said, frowning in an effort to make her thoughts clear, "Hart hated Alan. It was just a natural dislike from the start. So whenever the dog saw Alan, if it was at Bobbie's apartment or even on the street, that dog used to bite him. They say children and animals have an instinct about people. You can't fool an animal or a child. And that dog knew that man had something wrong with him. Every time Alan walked into the apartment the dog would hunch up and start to snarl . . . right away . . .

and then if Alan took one step the dog would hurl himself right on him and bite."

"I don't know about that."

"About what?"

"Instinct," Charlotte said. "There's nothing wrong with my character and Bobbie's dog always snarled at me, and it bit me a lot."

"Little baby bites," Mona said. "He never drew blood. He nipped me, too, a couple of times, but I probably scared him."

"That dog always tore my stockings," Charlotte said. "I remember now, that's why I didn't see Bobbie after a while. He bit children and old ladies in the park. They'd offer him a dog biscuit and he'd bite their hand, and then he'd get the biscuit, too, because they would drop it. If biting is a test of anybody's bad character, that dog is the one with the bad character."

"That's absolute nonsense," Mona said. "Hart is a high-strung dog. He's alone all day."

"He even bit Bobbie's mother."

"Well, he never bit Bobbie. That dog adored her."

"Now I forgot your story," Charlotte said.

"I'm getting to it. Anyway, nobody suspected there was anything wrong with Alan, because he was always so good to Bobbie. He even sent Bobbie's mother to Florida after she had that operation, and he paid for the whole thing. Three weeks and plane fare. Bobbie could have paid—she makes fifty an hour—

but he insisted. He said his parents died when he was very young and he never had a chance to do anything for them. Bobbie's mother's divorced, she doesn't have anybody but Bobbie, so Alan was always being nice. And he used to use pull at the agency he worked for to get Bobbie extra jobs, like ads, so she'd get really big. He knew she hated to go on location trips —they're a big bore and everybody thinks they're so glamorous—so he fixed it so she made enough money she didn't have to go away all year. Except, of course, the Paris collections. Even Bobbie was thrilled as a baby about doing the Paris collections.

"I wish I could do them. But Bobbie's really something special, as long as she keeps her weight down. She really has style. And she looks different in every picture, that's important. Oh, I remember one time Alan took her out to dinner with a friend of his from college, a guy from California or somewhere, and he told this other boy Bobbie was Turkish and didn't speak a word of English, so she sat there all night and didn't say a word, and the guy kept telling Alan how beautiful she was and how lucky he was, except was he sure he wanted to marry a girl he couldn't *communicate* with! Bobbie said it was a riot. But that night when they went home, she said it was the first time Alan acted peculiar. She said he got very depressed. There was no reason. He just kept staring at her, and then he asked her if she really thought she'd be happy with him. And she asked him what he meant, and he said that wasn't *really* what he'd meant at all. It doesn't sound peculiar when I say it, but she said it was very peculiar when it happened.

"Well, anyway, about a month after that, Bobbie had to go to Paris to do the collections, so she gave Alan the key to her apartment and asked him would he please go there every morning on his way to the office and walk the dog, and then stop by on his way home from work and walk him again and feed him. She left all the dog food and everything where Alan could find it. She couldn't take Hart to Paris with her because it takes so long for that stupid quarantine the poor puppy would have been locked up the whole time she was over there. And she couldn't stand to put him in a kennel. So, since Bobbie doesn't have a doorman, she simply had to ask Alan to do it.

"Actually, he was pretty nice about it. He said it would be like having a little bit of Bobbie for a souvenir while she was away. So she went to Paris.

"I didn't find out what happened until afterward, partly from Bobbie and partly, believe it or not, from Bobbie's mother. It seems Alan called Bobbie's mother afterward and tried to explain. He said he wasn't explaining for Bobbie's sake but for hers. Naturally he didn't ever plan to see Bobbie again. But he said he wanted to call her mother just this once to *explain* about what he called . . . temporary insanity. And Bobbie's mother *forgave* him! I don't know how he could have called it temporary insanity, because it was long-range, planned insanity, and you'd have to be pretty crazy to be crazy that long. He was temporarily insane for at least three days any way you look at it. I figured it out.

"Anyway, the first day after Bobbie left for Paris, Alan went into her apartment with the key—the lights were all on, of course, so Hart wouldn't get scared—and he opened a can of dog food and put it in Hart's bowl, and just as he was putting the bowl of food on the floor where Hart could get at it, Hart evidently snarled like he always does and bit Alan on the hand. Well, Alan ought to be used to that. It had happened hundreds of times. But I guess this time it was like the last straw. Alan said that was when he started to go temporarily insane.

"He put the leash on the dog and took him right out in the street without even letting the poor thing eat, and he kept walking and thinking about his life, and getting married to Bobbie, and all sorts of nutty things. He said it was like he was drowning and his life was passing before his eyes, only it was his future life, not his past. He walked until he got all the way downtown over on the West Side in some awful neighborhood, and there was a run-down brownstone with a sign in the window that said VETERINARIAN. He went inside with Hart in his arms, and he told the vet this was his poor, dear dog, who was dying in dreadful pain, and he couldn't stand to watch it any more. He asked the doctor to please put the dog to sleep.

"You can imagine the kind of quack who would do a thing like that . . . but the vet did it. Alan gave him

132

twenty-five dollars and said he was glad it had been so painless, and now he knew his dear dog was in Puppydog Heaven. So the vet asked did he want the dog cremated or buried, and Alan said, No, no, he wanted to take his dog to be buried in the family cemetery.

"He had the dead dog in his arms and he walked crosstown again until he got to Third Avenue where he remembered once he had noticed a taxidermist. You know, those Godawful places that have stuffed bears with glass eyes? He told the taxidermist that his darling dog had died, and he wanted to have him stuffed so he could keep him around the house always. So the taxidermist said, Fine, and would he like the dog in standing or sitting position?

"Alan said, Well, he and his darling dog used to play a game when the dog was alive, and he would like to have the dog preserved in the position he took for their game, so it would be a memento. He said the best way to describe it was as the Snarling Position.

"Two days later, he came back to the taxidermist and got the dog, all stuffed and lifelike in Snarling Position. Alan told the taxidermist it was a very artistic job and exactly the way he remembered the dog best. And then he took a cab to Bobbie's.

"He let himself into her apartment with the key and put Hart down in the entry hall. Then he turned out all the lights in the apartment except the ceiling light in the entry hall—the one that was shining down directly on the dog. The first thing Bobbie would see when she opened the door was that.

"Then he locked the door after himself and went downstairs and dropped the key into Bobbie's mailbox."

Mona shivered. "And that's the story. It still gives me cold chills . . . I mean, a poor, defenseless *dog!*"

"But—Bobbie—" Charlotte said. "What happened?"

"Well, she's getting married to a French photographer. As a matter of fact, she met him on that trip. He's crazy about dogs—has two of his own—so she wrote him about what Alan did to Hart, and then he wrote back, and . . . well, it worked out."

"Is she happy?"

"Radiant. Never saw her look better. She got hippy again because she hasn't been coming here, but she says she'll go on a diet in Paris."

"Fat chance."

"No, she's good at it. When she went on a diet last year she lost fourteen pounds."

"But, except for the hips, she looked pretty?"

"Marvelous."

"I'm glad," Charlotte said. "How's her mother?"

"Well, you know how cancer is. Bobbie said she went yesterday to visit her mother in the hospital, to tell her she was getting married, and her mother hardly recognized her."

"Shame."

"Yeah. Well . . ."

"I think I will go over to say *bon voyage* to Bobbie," Charlotte said. "I mean, who knows when we'll see her again?"

"I'll go with you. We'll bring her a bottle of champagne. Bobbie said she won't get back to America for at least a couple of years."

Trompe l'Oeil

THERE ARE very few crimes of passion in North America; it is neither our heritage nor our habit to be publicly passionate, even for an instant. There is an occasional scandal, but when all the evidence is assembled, the plot reveals itself as so elaborate, the weapons of destruction so profuse, that one wonders where, in all this guilty planning, there was time for passion at all. There is, of course, a sexual relationship in each of these tragedies. Since it is illicit, the outsiders like to imagine the relationship had some sort of superhuman emotional ferocity. So, in the end, one sometimes wonders whether the murderer was electrocuted for adultery or the adulterer was electrocuted for murder. In this temperate climate, the crime is passion itself.

In New York City, a thirty-year-old woman named

Evelyn Perry lived alone in a two-and-a-half-room apartment in a reconverted brownstone in the East Sixties. She was pleasant looking, with brown hair, hazel eyes, pale skin, and the kind of forgettable face that women often have when they have no discernible defects. People often told her she resembled Jeanne Crain, Deanna Durbin, Marisa Pavan, or "my best friend back home—but *exactly!*" She had come to New York eight years before from Omaha, Nebraska, where she still had parents and a younger sister who was married to a court stenographer.

For the first four years of her residence in New York, Evelyn Perry had shared an apartment with two other girls; not the same two girls, but a procession of them, who left to marry, to go home, or to live alone. She was employed as a secretary in the advertising department of a home-furnishings magazine, and finally, when she could afford it, she decided to get her own apartment. Solitary living seemed a more normal life, particularly since the supply of roommates was beginning to come from more and more casual sources, such as the friend of a friend; the last roommate had moved on with most of Evelyn Perry's clothes in her suitcases.

The first year of living by herself was a new pleasure: the cleanliness, the quiet, the independence, the acquisition of pretty things that belonged to no one else. *My* red casserole, to cook *my* chicken rosemary, for *my* supper. But it was a phase of delight that gradually paled. The second step was entertaining friends.

After a year, this, too, lost its glittering bridal quality, since she had few friends, and eventually it seemed more like dredging up the nightly nourishment for the family than like giving a party. It was a Cinderella family that vanished at midnight.

Often, as she approached thirty, it occurred to Evelyn Perry that her couch, which converted into a double bed with a single pillow at the center of the headboard, was less a sign of solitary luxury than a marker of defeat. It did not mean that she was celibate; it simply meant that this bed was not a place where two people slept together at night. Love was investigation, search, indiscretion, stimulation, or even, occasionally, embarrassing boredom, but never what she wanted it to be. All the years passed as one, divided only by the seasons and names of semi-annual lovers.

More and more, during the winter of her eighth career year in New York, she felt she was drawing into herself—waiting, hovering, as self-contained and blind as a flower wrapped in its bud. Around her was quiet, loneliness, and within was a rage of color and life that was hardly aware of its own existence. That other life erupted in dreams which were forgotten in the morning, their colors trailing off into fragments like one petal left on the bedclothes.

❧

EVELYN PERRY rode the Lexington Avenue bus reading the morning tabloids, she ate lunch in the restau-

rant in her office building, and at night she stopped
off at a grocery store to buy her supper. On Saturdays
and Sundays she cleaned her apartment, quietly,
painstakingly, picking a dead match out of a clean
ashtray, folding the bath towels on their racks so all
the edges were tucked inside. On Sunday mornings
she closed up her convertible bed and arranged the
cushions neatly upon it; on Sunday nights she opened
it again, unseen by anyone but herself all through the
day, and went to sleep. This life was not restful; she
burned from within, but she looked pale, and she
was not pretty. This burning within the soul does not
make a princess of anyone, despite romantic notions
to the contrary; the eyes grow dull from gazing in-
ward at the holocaust.

On the long, quiet evenings during the week, Evelyn Perry's favorite place had become, for a peculiar
reason, her kitchen. The kitchen of this apartment,
like the kitchens of many New York apartments, was
so tiny and cramped that in order to make it bearable
she had installed a device to deceive and please the
eye: *trompe l'oeil* wallpaper on the far wall, depicting
a scene as if viewed from a small balcony. Working
at a home-furnishings magazine, she had been able to
buy the paper wholesale; it was very expensive and
the view almost looked real. The scene was the curving beach and varicolored sea of Copacabana Beach
in Rio de Janeiro. In the distance were misty purple
mountains. Closer up were white, modern apartment
buildings in a row along the curve of pale sand. To

complete the illusion of space and air, she had hired a carpenter to make a shelf jutting out from the printed railing, as if it were a little table on the balcony, and she could sit at this shelf or table and dine facing the sea. It was such a realistic and refreshing scene that one never got the impression one was merely sitting like a punished child facing the wall.

The one detail the artist had forgotten was people. It was a beach without inhabitants, a Robinson Crusoe beach in the middle of a busy resort city. But it was easy enough to imagine, in the mornings while she drank her coffee before rushing off to work, that it was still too early for anyone to come to the beach, and at night she could pretend it was too late. She pretended that she lived in one of those white, tall apartment houses, perhaps on a low floor where she was closer to the brightness of life, and this was her balcony and each morning was the start of her day in Rio. She would be working in a little office somewhere, and on weekends she would swim and lie in the sun. She would not be lonely because there would be many foreigners in the city, and they would all speak to her, being as lonely as she was. There would be ardent Latin men.

She had read a few articles about Brazil in fashion magazines, and one day she bought an elementary Portuguese instruction book, because it seemed to open up that world a little more. She studied the book (instead of her tabloids) on the bus in a desultory manner. Then at night she would sit in her kitchenette with the ceiling light off, one lamp lighted in the living room at her back, and she would gaze down at that beach and sea, all silvered in the moonlight.

Everything was still. The surf at the edge of the white sand was white, too, and lifted in the air like blown lace. There were little lights glittering in the buildings. She wondered if people were having parties, there in those lighted rooms. Below, on the sand, she saw small shapes that might have been lovers wandering there by the edge of the ocean under the stars.

At night the world had its own mysterious life; fish swam in the sea, invisible but living, and people moved in those dark, hidden streets, hand in hand. Life waited for her in the darkness. Looking down from her balcony, Evelyn Perry felt her scalp prickle; at the roots of her hair there was a chill that spread through her whole body. She felt a terrible poignance as she leaned there on her railing under the sky, as insignificant as anyone who had ever stared out at night at the curve of the universe. Hours passed at times, and she did not move, watching the lovers on the sand and the great world above them; and when she went to bed, she slept immediately and deeply.

At the office during the day, she was quiet. She had never liked her job; it was boring, and she had been at the same desk for eight years. She could do most of her typing without thinking. Some days she folded circulars and put them into envelopes. In the evenings she came directly home from the office in the winter's early darkness to the summer beneath her balcony.

There was a certain couple who came to the beach often at night, sometimes twice a week. They arrived separately at a designated place below, met furtively, and did not stay more than an hour. The woman was well dressed and lovely, the man tall and strong, and their encounters passionate. She wondered sometimes if it was her right to watch something so personal, lurking there jealously in the semi-darkness. Was there not something obscene, something both pathetic and vile, about a Peeping Tom? But what about exhibitionists? If people paraded their passions on the beach, they could not expect privacy, even in the moonlight. For the first time, the enormity of her loneliness overwhelmed her, and she clenched her fists against her eyes, shuddering, and wept without tears. Useless and lonely, lonely, lonely . . . dulled with uselessness and habit, waiting without anticipation.

When she looked down again, the couple on the beach were arguing, standing face to face in the awkward, stubborn postures of people who are shouting at each other. She watched them dully, wondering why lovers were stupid enough to fight. How ugly they were, braced in anger! The woman turned away and began to run, and the man followed her, stopping her with both his arms. The woman twisted away and struck him, and then he strangled her. It was as simple as that. His hands joined around her neck, he stiffened, she struggled and then was still. He laid her on the sand as gently as if she were asleep, looked down at her for a long moment as with surprise, and began to cry. Then he fled into the darkness.

Staring after him, Evelyn Perry wondered with horror if the tide would come up and take the woman's body into the sea. She felt ill. She rose and went away from the scene, quickly, dazed, into her own warm apartment, into her own quiet life; but she could not make the image of the murder leave the back of her eyes, and that night, for the first time, Evelyn Perry did not sleep at all.

The next day was Saturday, so she did not go to the office. Preparing her eggs and toast in the morning, Evelyn Perry avoided looking at her wallpaper, but then, when she unavoidably had to glance at it, it seemed so artificial and harmless that she had to smile. This was New York, not Rio; the eye could be deceived by the mind, but the mind could be made impervious to its own horrors. For the first time in weeks she would go shopping, she would get out of the house. But she was taken with torpor, and as the day went by she found many tiresome things that had to be done before she could leave; it was important to wipe out the slivers of soap from the soap dish in the bathroom, for instance. When she was dressed, and all the vacuuming had been done, it was four o'clock, too late to begin an expedition in the stores because the salesgirls would be tired and nasty, the customers pushing anxiously to get home with their bundles. She had not even gone out for the newspapers, but it seemed too difficult an effort. She felt detached. The petty blown-up scandals and exposés of her tabloids bored her, they seemed so temporary to anyone who was not involved. Dusk came early.

It was pleasant to eat supper on her balcony, watching the lights come on in the buildings along the beach. She resented the thought that the telephone might ring, that anyone might call her away from this hour of privacy before the night. But the telephone never rang on weekend evenings; she was safe. She wondered what had happened to the body of the strangled woman during the day. If a child playing on the beach had discovered it, the child might be emotionally scarred for life. She wondered whether the dead woman had children of her own. Had she been a married woman to be so furtive, or had it been her lover who was married? Gazing down at the spot where the lovers had quarreled, Evelyn Perry saw a man walking along the beach very slowly, with his head lowered. He stopped where the body had lain and suddenly threw himself down full length on the sand, lying there on his face as if he were dead. Then she saw that he was crying. He lay there for a long time until the sky became completely dark. Then he stood up painfully, wiped his face with a handkerchief and went away. So two men had loved her, Evelyn Perry thought.

She wondered who this other man was. Not the father; he seemed too young. Not a brother; could grief so intense and intimate be for a relative? He must have been the husband, the *cornudo,* who had lost his wife long before that tragic night. Perhaps, if he had known his wife had a lover, Evelyn Perry thought, he would have strangled her himself, and it would have been the lover who would be grieving tonight.

The beach seemed lonely without the lovers. There were other tiny dark shapes in the distance but they did not matter; they were strangers. She did not want to look any more, and that night, when she went to bed, she found herself weeping on her pillow for a dead woman she had never actually known.

On Sunday afternoon, just before sunset in summertime Rio, when it was already dark in winterbound New York, Evelyn Perry saw two policemen in khaki uniforms escorting the widowed husband back to the scene of the crime. They were pulling him and he was protesting, trying to get away. He was handcuffed to one of them. The poor man, she thought, first the other thing, now this. It isn't fair. But what was fair? It seemed enormously fair that life should be so unjust, that the wrong person should always suffer for the wrong crime instead of the one he had committed. Those guilty of omission shall be punished, those guilty of commission shall go free.

As soon as she had thought this she was immediately ashamed of herself. It was not life that was unfeeling, it was people themselves. She was as much to blame as the next one. She was the witness to that crime on the beach, and if she spoke up the innocent man would be freed.

She ran into her living room looking desperately for pencil and paper and her Portuguese instruction book with the dictionary in the back. She found a sheet of typing paper, larger than stationery, and brought the things to the kitchen. Hurriedly, her hands shaking, she looked for the proper words. Lover . . . there was no word for lover in a foreign-language instruction book. *Senhor, senhora,* but never lover. She remembered her high-school Latin and applied it to Portuguese: *amante. O amante.* There was not even any word for kill. Call the maid, there is a fly in my bedroom. But no word for kill the fly. Call a doctor. Call the police. *The lover did it.* That was the closest she could come, so she printed the words on the large piece of white paper and, with cellophane tape, attached it to her balcony railing so that it faced the beach.

It was too late; the policemen had already left, dragging the accused. Evelyn Perry had never felt so useless in her life. But the sign was there. She would leave it, and perhaps tomorrow they would return, or perhaps someone else would see it and tell the police. The case would have to be a scandal, people would be talking about it, and someone would be sure to see her sign and tell the police. *O amante o cometeu.* They would know it was the lover who killed the woman; they would know.

The next day, Evelyn Perry did not go to the office. She wanted to go, she did not want to go; three times during the night she leaned from her bed to push the bell-switch of her alarm clock, and later to pull it out again. Her only excuse for irresponsibility was responsibility: she was not important at the office—someone else could stuff circulars into envelopes—but she might be important here. She had to admit she was curious. She felt guilty about staying away from the office, and then she felt resentful of the tiresome conscience that made her feel guilty. She could not help looking forward to daylight.

But then, when she was walking about her apartment looking for things to do, bewildered by these hours of unplanned and unexpected leisure, she was not quite sure why she had stayed at home after all. The *trompe l'oeil* wallpaper in her kitchen was flat and painted, even though cleverly conceived, and the piece of white paper taped to the wall with the imprint of her writing faintly showing through from the other side so embarrassed her that, although she could not bear to tear it down, she did use this blank side to write her grocery list. She napped fitfully on the bed turned back into a couch, and she told herself this day was therapy for an overtired mind. But she was so nervous by five o'clock that she got up to brew a pot of tea which she did not really want, and then let it get cold on the drainboard while she looked out at the beach and the slowly shadowing sky.

It was twilight, the true moment when the day is divided in two. Noon does not count as a division, nor does midnight; they are only hours of the clock. But twilight separates the lonely from the loved. The lonely leave their busy offices and go away from people, the loved finish their work and prepare to be with their families or sweethearts. Evelyn Perry, who had been one of the former, now found herself standing at her balcony after a day of leisure, watching the people below and wondering which of them were aimless and which ones were hurrying. Finally the beach was empty. The bathers were gone, the lovers not yet arriving. She saw a tall man walking alone along the edge of the sea.

The man stopped near where the woman had been killed and looked around. He looked up then at Evelyn Perry standing lighted on her balcony, and she looked down at him. It was the lover, the murderer. He glanced at her with disinterest, as one glances momentarily at any stranger on a balcony, and she saw that he had grown haggard and tense. He held himself warily, poised for flight, like an animal. One arm embraced a rifle in a curve so unfamiliar and graceless that she knew this rifle was the companion of the hunted, not the hunter. He looked about him in a crazed way, as if the mourning and waiting of the past three days had driven him out of his senses.

Then she felt sorry for him because he was as

much a sacrifice as the murdered girl or the husband. He looked at her again, at her balcony rather, and she saw his face fully. She saw the look on his face gradually changing from curiosity to comprehension and then horror as he read the sign she had taped to her balcony railing.

She did not feel afraid. He was so tiny, so far below, that she felt almost godlike in that moment on her balcony, right but regretful, huge, illumined, standing beside her handprinted message of doom. The rifle he held was only the size of a toothpick. When he lifted it to his shoulder she felt surprised, even amused, more regretful than ever because he was so pathetic and small. She was frightened only when she felt the unexpected instant of overwhelming pain.

After Evelyn Perry had not been to her office all week and had not answered her telephone, someone called her landlady, who entered the unruffled apartment and found the body. The landlady did not know the name of Evelyn Perry's doctor, so she called her own. Death had occurred Monday evening between five and six o'clock. The autopsy did not show the cause of death, but an autopsy never reveals barbiturate poisoning, which is usually suspected first in cases of this kind. Since there was neither a suicide note nor an empty bottle lying nearby, a chemical analysis was taken from the vital organs, but that did not show anything either. No one ever really knew how Evelyn Perry died, but there did not seem to be any reason to imagine she had been killed. She was nobody's unwanted wife, nor was she carrying an unwanted child, nor was she anyone's unwanted mistress. She was certainly not the sort of person anyone would want very badly to get out of his life.

Rima The Bird Girl

I DON'T remember the day we first met, but my first memory of her is of a wraithlike dark-haired girl sitting in the corner of the living room of our dormitory at college, reciting poetry—no, almost shouting it—she and a friend in unison. And it seemed to me then as if poetry should always be shouted in this inspired, almost orgiastic, way, for it was really music. "O love is the crooked thing,/There is nobody wise enough/To find out all that is in it, . . . Ah, penny, brown penny, brown penny,/One cannot begin it too soon."

Her name was Rima Allen, and she came from a small town in Pennsylvania which had neither the distinction of being a grimy coal town nor Main Line, but just a town. Her mother had been reading

Green Mansions when her daughter was born, and she felt it would give her child some individuality to be named Rima. Her father was a tax accountant, a vague man who spent his life bent over records of other people's lives. He thought Rima was a silly name, but his wife overruled him, and later it was she who chose Radcliffe for Rima, and so we met.

There was a fireplace at one end of the living room in our dormitory, and beside it a nook, wood paneled and cushioned in velvet. Rima was sitting in that nook with her temporary friend, a lumpy debutante from New York who powdered her face like a Kabuki dancer and had once brought a copy of the Social Register into dinner to point out her own name in it. This frightened and graceless snob (whose registered name I have forgotten) was the last person on earth you would expect to find chanting Yeats with such obvious joy, yet Rima had made her memorize dozens of his poems. I knew at once that Rima was a special girl, a girl people gravitated toward to find their dream, their opposite, whatever it was they could not find alone.

"An aged man is but a paltry thing,/A tattered coat upon a stick, unless/Soul clap its hands and sing, and louder sing/For every tatter in its mortal dress."

Rima was a tall girl who always looked very small and fragile, until you noticed her standing next to someone else and realized with surprise that she was big. She had narrow shoulders and small bones, a delicate way of moving, and a soft, child's voice. Her face, in those years of our late teens, was a white blur, as I suppose all our faces were, for we did not yet know who we were. I have a photograph of her sitting on the library steps, a pretty, pale, no-face child of seventeen, all wonder, her arms held out to the wan New England sun.

Every one of us owned several bottles of cologne; Rima had none, but she had one bottle of perfume. We all had many party dresses; Rima had only one, but it was orange, with a swirly skirt, and it had cost a hundred dollars. I remember her always hiding in her room, the shades down, studying, or reading the poetry she loved, and then the sound of the phone bell . . . and ten minutes later she emerged—a swirl of orange skirt, a cloud of Arpege drifting after her, as if she had suddenly been told she existed.

That's all I remember of her from those days; it was, after all, fifteen years ago, and her story had not begun. When we graduated, four of us went to Washington to work in offices, share a house, and find husbands. I had been a zoology major in college, studying such unfeminine things as mollusks, but when we went to Washington I decided to become a secretary along with the others, because we were almost twenty-one and not getting any younger. Everyone knew you found nothing among the mollusks but shells and a lot of ugly old men. We had decided on Washington instead of New York because the other two girls said that was where the bright young men were. A few months after the four of us settled in rooms in a Greek Revival style mansion turned into a rooming house, the two who had brought us to this city of romance began going steady with two boys they had known back at Harvard, and I realized why we had come.

I missed zoology and hated typing and filing; but missing one's work takes an odd form in girls, I think —I was less conscious of the loss than I was of what replaced it, a ferocious need to be loved. I needed someone to inflict all that creative energy on, it didn't matter much who. Of the four of us, it was only Rima who seemed to enjoy being a secretary; who preferred staying home and listening to old Noel Coward records to going out with a new prospect; who went to bed early and got up early, eagerly, without resentment; and who went to the office in her prettiest clothes. I soon discovered it was because she was in love with someone she had met at work.

It was one of those impossibly romantic meetings that occur only in bad movies and real life. The man was attached to the State Department, one of those career diplomats whose work is so important and confidential that you can talk to him for an hour at a cocktail party and realize afterward he has not said a word about himself. He was American, forty-five years old, very attractive, totally sophisticated and, of course, married. Rima had been dispatched to take some papers to his office. There she was, in the doorway—his secretary was in the powder room—and he was alone behind the largest desk she had ever seen. She looked at him, knowing only vaguely who he was and how important he was, thinking only that he was a grownup and extraordinarily attractive. She was wearing her neat little college-girl suit, her hair tied back with a ribbon, her face all admiration and awe. She thought as girls do in the darkness of movie theaters without any sense of further reality: I'd love to go out with him! No one knows what he thought. But the next day he took her to the country for lunch.

She did not tell me who her mysterious lover was for several months, and she never told our other two roommates at all. She saved newspaper clippings about glittering Washington parties he had attended, but because diplomatic amours are very diplomatic in Washington, she had little else in the way of souvenirs, not even a matchbook from a restaurant. I did not know how they managed to meet during those first few months, but I always knew when she was meeting him because again, as in our college days, there was a swirl of brightly colored skirt running down the stairs, a faint cloud of perfume (Joy this time instead of Arpege), and the air around her was charged with life. When she finally told me his name, it was only after they had both decided they were in love.

Rima had had crushes on boys at Harvard, had even cried over a few missed phone calls, but it was nothing like this. As for him, he had played around with little interest with a few predatory wives, but he had never had a real love affair with anyone since his marriage. Rima was so young, so full of confidence in a future in which she would always be young and he would always care for her, that she never even thought of asking him to get a divorce. It was a courtship. They planned how they would meet, when they would meet, how she could see him most often, how she could get along. He could not bear for her to be poor; even the thought that she was spending part of her $60 salary on taxis to meet him appalled him, he wanted to make everything up to her, but how? She refused to go out with any of the boys (we still called them that) who phoned, and he knew it. Suddenly, one day, our freezer was full of steaks, the refrigerator was filled with splits of champagne, and our house was so filled with flowers I thought someone had died.

I went with Rima one day to help her sell her jewelry so that she could buy him a birthday present. Her charm bracelet with the gold disk that said "Sweet Sixteen," her college ring . . . whatever she could not sell she pawned. None of it meant anything to her. "I want to get him gold cuff links," she said. "He wears French cuffs." I thought of the O. Henry story about the gift of the Magi, but it was not the same, because he was not giving up anything for her, and what she was giving up for him was only bits of metal and chips of gems that belonged to an already fading past.

That summer, when our first year of independence drew to a close, our two roommates married the boys they had come to Washington to pursue, and Rima and I had two whole rooms to ourselves. Summers in Washington are very hot. An air conditioner mysteriously appeared in our bedroom window, installed by a man from the air-conditioning company whom neither of us had sent for. On the first cool fall day, for the first time, I was allowed to meet the diplomat. He came to our house for tea and sat on the edge of one of our frayed chairs, very elegant in his hand-tailored suit and Sulka tie. He even wore a vest. I thought he looked like our uncle; not our father—he was too young, too glamorous, too much from another world. But there was something fatherly in the way he looked around at our landlady's furniture with amusement and yet a little annoyance—was it clean enough, good enough, for his child?—the way he smiled with adult pride at everything Rima said, as if she were a precious being from another planet. I could hardly believe any of this was happening; I think, in a way, neither could he. Yet they were obviously in love with each other.

He went to New York on several business trips that fall and winter and took Rima with him, meeting her as if by accident on the train, where he had taken a private bedroom for the short trip and Rima had a ticket in the parlor car. They had rooms in the same hotel on different floors. At Buccellati's he bought her a gold and emerald ring, which she wore on her left hand, but they entered and left the shop by the back door. When they returned to Washington after the last trip, his wife met him at the station, and Rima alighted from a different car and stood staring on the station platform as her love drove off in a silver-gray foreign automobile with someone who was suddenly flesh and blood, an actuality, a force, a monster.

"I saw her, the old hag," Rima said to me that night, almost in tears. "I wish I could kill her. She's very sophisticated . . . she was wearing a real Chanel suit, and the Chanel shoes and bag too . . . she's too thin, she chain-smokes and uses a holder . . . she's one of those terribly chic, tense women who knows everybody and always says and does the right things. You could tell. She's unhappy, though . . . she must know he loves someone else. Women as nervous as that always know they aren't loved. He told me he doesn't love her any more. He'd leave her if it weren't for his career; a scandal—zip!" She drew her finger across her throat. "He's so proper and old-fashioned in his way, nobody is like him any more. If it weren't for her he could marry me and we'd both be happy. I hate her, the old hag."

"She doesn't sound like an old hag," I said.

"She is!"

"All right, she is."

"And ugly, too."

"Well, at least she's ugly."

"No, she's not ugly," Rima said. "I wish she were.

She must have something if he won't leave her for me. If he really didn't love her, he'd leave her, no matter what he says. How could he marry me? I couldn't be a hostess, I couldn't run two homes the way she does. I don't know anything about being a diplomat's wife. I *know* he loves me, but he won't leave *her*. . . ."

So she did want to marry him after all. It had been inevitable. The courtship had been beautiful; the five-minute meetings in hallways, the stolen afternoons and weekends—all had been part of the discovery and wonder of love. But after a year and a half the champagne of secrecy had gone flat. I suspected that Rima had wanted to marry him long before this but had never dared say the words until she saw his wife and realized bitterly that someone had married him, someone was sharing all of his life except those stolen afternoons; for someone it was possible.

All lovers make near-fatal mistakes in their relationships; it is part of the pleasure of love, illicit or not, to tempt providence. So when, one weekend when his wife was away, the diplomat took Rima to his home, it seemed to me merely one of the fatal mistakes some lovers have to make. It was not fatal in any immediate sense, for they were not caught, no one saw them, the servants were away, his wife did not return unexpectedly with a detective or a gun. On his part, it was only a further avowal of his love for Rima; he wanted her to see where and how he lived, he didn't want her to be an outsider. He wanted her to approve of him, of the beautiful things with which he filled his life. He wanted to give her a setting to picture when she dreamed of him, a background for her lonely fantasies; perhaps he also wanted to be able to imagine her in his home when she was no longer there and he was sitting through a dull diplomatic dinner party. The mistake was fatal because Rima did approve of his home . . . she approved of it too much.

She told me about it that night in detail, and I could picture her scampering through those huge rooms like a child, touching each piece of antique furniture as her lover told her what famous person might have sat in this chair, dined from that plate (now an ashtray), or what skill distinguished the weaving of this piece of cloth from any other. She peered into every closet, learning about the heirloom silver, the china, the crystal; she even tried on some of his wife's clothes. To him, Rima was a child, wistful, amusing, and filled with amazement, so he let her try on the Chanels, the Diors, stroke the furs, wave the lapis cigarette holder in the air as if it held a cigarette and she were a grownup at the ball. When she returned home to the Greek Revival rooming house, the photographic mind that had gotten *A*'s at Radcliffe was a living archive of memorabilia.

The bulging scrapbooks of souvenirs and photographs from our college days, which still amused us on Sunday afternoons, were shipped home to her parents. In their place appeared glossy magazines that looked more like books, with names like "Antiquaries," and "A History of Battersea Boxes." One of them was even in French. The diplomat collected Battersea boxes, and also tiny silver boxes with crests on them, so Rima began to scour back street antique shops for a collection exactly like his. Real Battersea boxes were too expensive, but on her twenty-third birthday the diplomat gave her one, topped with white china, on which was written in fine script: "A Trifle From a Friend."

"He wanted to give me a coat," she told me, "but this coat will go another year. I just had to have a real Battersea box."

There was a one-of-a-kind pair of Louis XV chairs in the diplomat's living room. But there turned out to be, surprisingly, an identical pair, for Rima discovered it on a trip to New York, and she began putting away part of her salary every month to buy them. "A hundred dollars a month forever. . . ." Our landlady's frayed chairs were sent to the basement, and the two Louis XV chairs took their place in front of our fireplace that December, for the diplomat had added the frighteningly large difference for a Christmas present. But he seemed disappointed with the gift she had chosen for him to give her, because he surprised her with an additional present, a beige and white fox fur coat. She looked young and rich and daring in the coat, but as for the chairs, I was afraid to sit on them.

One night Rima packed all her career-girl clothes in a large box and sent them to charity, for she was the new owner of a real Chanel suit with the shoes and bag to match. She bought a cigarette holder and began to smoke; she said it would help her lose weight, for she had suddenly decided she was too fat. When her lover told her she was getting too thin, she cried all night, but she did not stop smoking, for the excuse was it would help her stop biting her nails. The collection of tiny silver boxes with crests grew larger and covered the entire top of a spindly-legged antique table Rima had found, which was by coincidence exactly like the one in the bedroom of the diplomat and his wife. The real Chanel suit was joined, in a few months, by another, and a white Dior evening gown, which Rima wore at home in the evening, alone, while she sipped sherry from a certain crystal wineglass, chain-smoked, and wrote letters to a certain firm in Paris asking if it was possible to obtain ten yards of a certain brocaded fabric which had been specially made at one time for another American client, and a tiny sample of which she happened to have snipped from the under-side of that client's sofa.

When the fabric finally arrived, the sofa it would cover had arrived too, a gift for Rima's twenty-fourth birthday. I reminded her we were still paying rent for a furnished apartment, although it now looked like a museum, and our landlady's basement looked like a warehouse. Rima looked at me with the nervous, near-tearful look she had acquired during the past year, which somehow made her look rather tragic and mysterious. "We're too old to live like pigs any more," she said. "Don't you want a real home?"

I did, and I wanted something more, something elusive but wonderful, which I felt must surely be beyond the next corner, or at the next party, or on the threshold of our front door tomorrow night. . . . It had to be, or I felt I would disappear. So one fall evening, when the doorbell rang, announcing the arrival of perhaps the hundredth blind date I would have had in Washington, I decided: If he's anything better than a monster, whoever he is, *this one* I will fall in love with.

He was far from a monster, and he had green eyes and a sense of humor—my two fatal weaknesses —so while he sat in my living room talking and trying to make me like him he never knew he needn't have bothered, because I already loved him. He talked all night, and at dawn, when he remembered he had invited me to his apartment after dinner to make a pass at me, and now it was too late because it was day and we had to go to our offices, he decided he was in love with me, too.

"How could I not love you?" he asked (this young man who was already destined to become my first husband). "You are me. If I didn't love you, it would be like not loving myself."

My decision to marry him seemed as mad and romantic as my decision to fall in love with him. We were in his car at the curb in front of a restaurant. It was that first night, before his apartment, at our first restaurant together, the first time I had been in his car. I wanted to invent some test for destiny, something simple, arbitrary and irrevocable, therefore magic. "If he comes around to my side to open the door, I'll marry him. If he doesn't, he'll never know." He came around to open the door.

Rima gave a cocktail party for us when we announced our engagement, one of many parties she had begun to give. She had become a polished hostess, entertaining a mélange of people: minor politicians, intellectuals, an artist, a writer, an actress, a few foreigners who spoke no English at all but whose languages Rima had studied in college and perfected during the past few years of her diplomatic education. Her diplomat was not there, of course, and she had hidden her half-dozen tiny framed photographs of him in the dresser drawer, but his presence hovered in the rooms throughout the party, for it was now his home, done in his taste, filled with the objects of his pleasures, and the hostess who presided over it all with infinite charm might as well have been his wife. I had a brief irreverent fantasy of the diplomat coming here one night by accident, and panicking, not knowing which home he had come to.

At the party there was a visitor from New York, a young advertising executive. He was thirty-four, married twelve years to his high school sweetheart, and had two children. He was in Washington on business and obviously had never seen anyone like Rima at such close range. He was almost childishly infatuated with her after ten minutes. She flirted with him, named him Heathcliff (for that was rather whom he resembled), and although she obviously enjoyed playing with him, she seemed unaware of her new power. When she was moving about the room talking to her other guests he did not take his eyes off her.

"You need some more champagne, Heathcliff," Rima said, touching his arm lightly as she drifted past. "I want you to get good and drunk. 'Wine comes in at the mouth and love comes in at the eye; That's all we shall know for truth before we grow old and die.'"

"'I lift the glass to my mouth,'" he finished, "'I look at you, and I sigh.'"

She stopped dead and stared at him.

He smiled. There was something about him both boyish and wire-strong, a man who would piously refuse to deceive anyone and yet who was destined to deceive many people throughout his life because they would mistake him for someone simple. He raised his champagne glass at Rima. "'A mermaid found a swimming lad, picked him for her own, pressed her body to his body, laughed; and plunging down forgot in cruel happiness that even lovers drown.'"

"I don't think anyone could drown you," she said. "Heathcliff. . . ."

"Lady Brett Ashley. . . ." he said, transfixed.

"Me?" Rima laughed. "*Me?*"

He asked her to have dinner with him, as he was alone in this city, but she refused, explaining that she was in love with someone and never went out with anyone else.

"Where is he?" the advertising man asked, looking around the crowded room.

"He's not here."

"Oh. Married."

"Aren't you?" she replied sweetly, and drifted away to her guests.

My husband's work took him to New York, where we lived in a three-room apartment that I cleaned carefully every day. I went to the grocery store, read his magazines, his books, played his records, and waited for him to come home to eat the dinners I cooked. He did not like his work very much, and I did not work at all, so in the evenings we talked about the past, our childhoods, our friends; and when we were bored with that we talked about the future, although that seemed more like a game than reality. Sometimes we talked about Rima, who he said was neurotic. He said her life was going to end badly. "If I weren't married to you, I would save her from that man."

"Really? What makes you think she'd want you?" And at that moment, only six months after we had vowed to stay together forever, I wondered why I wanted him, either. I was beginning to look the way Rima had: nervous, lost, a bird girl who appeared out of a tree in the jungle to answer someone's dream and then disappeared at dawn . . . or was it he who disappeared, back into the real world, while the bird girl waited, invisible, for his return, for his summons, for her moments of reality?

Rima wrote to me quite regularly during those months. She had nothing else to do in the evenings, for the decorating job on her apartment was completed, and for some reason the diplomat was not seeing her as often as he used to. He was overworked, she wrote to me, and when he did manage a little time with her he usually spent it falling asleep.

"For the first time in my life," she wrote, "I feel old. I feel like a wife. But I want to marry him, and I know this isn't what our life would be like if I were really his wife. Then we'd share everything. But now he acts as if it isn't a romance any more. I don't know why. Do you remember in the beginning, when the house was full of flowers? He hasn't taken me out to lunch in four months."

They had their first serious fight. "He called me extravagant, said I cared too much about clothes," Rima wrote. "He used to tell me she was extravagant (the old hag) and I told him never to dare compare me with her. He said, 'In some ways you are like her,' and the way he said it was like an insult. He refused to explain. What more does he want from me? I can't be perfect, I need love, I can't help that. Why can't he love me enough to leave her? What's wrong with me that he can't love me enough to choose me over someone he doesn't love at all?"

The day after her fifth anniversary with the diplomat, Rima arrived at my apartment in New York. It seems they had been planning their fifth anniversary celebration for months; she had saved for and bought a new white Dior gown, had her hair done at eight in the morning in order to be at the office on time, and then at five o'clock—an hour before they were to meet to celebrate—he had phoned to say he had to go to an important dinner party, his wife would not understand if she had to attend alone, there was nothing he could do. Rima had gotten tremendously drunk on the bottle of Taittinger Blanc de Blancs 1953 she had been chilling in her refrigerator, given the Malossol caviar to the cleaning woman, thrown the white Dior on the closet floor, and taken the morning train to New York. He had promised to make it up to her, perhaps even a whole weekend away somewhere . . . but she could not wait.

"Wait!" she cried to me, tears pouring down her face as if she were a marble statue in a fountain. "Wait! Wait! All I have ever done is wait."

When my husband came home he flirted with Rima all evening—to save her?—as if I were invisible, and she took an instant dislike to it. When he started to talk about a girl he had known before he met me, Rima stood up. "If I ever get married," she said coldly, "my husband will never talk about other women in my presence. Nor will he ever flirt with other women when I am in the room. It's insulting. I am going to be first in his life, not just something that's *there*, and if I ever find there's someone else I'm going to leave."

"Isn't that a little too much to ask of a man?" I said, wishing I had her courage.

"It's what I will ask," Rima said.

"Well, Rima," he said, cheerfully nasty, "you ought to know."

I don't remember her ever speaking to my husband again, for that was the way Rima was. She drifted in and out of rooms during the two days she stayed with us, graceful and silent as a cat, always pleasant, but whenever he began to talk she suddenly wasn't there. The afternoon of the second day, when she was feeling repentant toward the diplomat, who did not know where she had gone, I went with Rima to Gucci's where she bought him a wallet. It was elegant, expensive, and impersonal—no, thank you, she would not wait to have it initialed—the kind of gift one had to give a man whose wife noticed all his personal possessions. Coming out of the store we saw the advertising man who had been at Rima's party, or rather, he saw us, for she did not recognize him.

He was so excited he called out to stop us; he shook her gloved hand with both his hands, and then he blushed, as if he had attacked her in my presence. Rima laughed, and then he laughed, too, and invited us both for a drink.

We went to the Plaza (Rima's choice), where Heathcliff had one Scotch (his limit, he told us) and Rima had champagne. She was wearing the beige and white fox coat over a pale wool dress, she had a long gold cigarette holder, her beige alligator handbag and the little package from Gucci were on the table, and she did indeed look like Lady Brett Ashley, or someone equally golden and fictional. We sat in the dark wood-paneled room, watching the sunset through the windows that overlooked the park, laughing, happy; and I thought that people from out of town who saw her here must be thinking she was a real New Yorker, on her way somewhere exciting for the evening. The advertising man evidently thought so, too, when he got up reluctantly, almost jealously, to catch his train to Old Greenwich.

There was a row of taxis at the curb. He helped us into the first, gave her a mischievous look and kissed her hand. When their eyes met, I had the feeling he had done some investigating about her friend in Washington. As we watched him walk away to the second taxi he seemed to change, grow firmer, more stubborn, as if preparing himself for an everyday life he had momentarily forgotten.

"He makes me feel young," Rima said wistfully. She smiled. "He makes me want to go to the country and throw snowballs."

She went back to Washington that night, and we did not see each other again until spring. In the meantime I had gotten what is known as a friendly divorce, and custody of the three-room apartment. There had been only two short letters from Rima during the intervening months. The first said, "I'm too depressed to write, everything is lousy."

The second said, "I have begun to realize that people don't break up because of one unforgivable incident, but rather, because of hopelessness. I used to think love could be killed with a mortal blow, but that's not true. Love goes on and on, until one day you wake up and realize that the hopelessness is stronger than the love. I've done everything I could think of, and it was not enough. He sees me once a week, for twenty minutes. How many more ways can I change? He says he loves me, but somehow that doesn't mean anything any more; they're just words. I hear them and I don't remember what they used to mean."

One morning Rima packed all her clothes and the collection of tiny antique boxes, and left Washington forever. She did not say goodbye to the diplomat, she simply disappeared into the dawn. She left every stick of antique furniture—his, hers, theirs, whatever it was—and I imagine the rooms in the Greek Revival style mansion must have looked very strange, as if the occupant had only gone out for a walk. She came to stay with me, and the first thing she did was give me her precious collection.

"I remember you used to admire them. Just consider them a house gift."

The second thing she did was get another secretarial job, because she insisted on paying half the rent. I had decided to go back to zoology and was taking a Master's degree at night and working days as a receptionist so I could study my textbooks behind the potted plant that stood on my glossy desk. I was much happier than I had expected to be. Rima surprised me by her resiliency. I had resigned myself nervously to having to nurse a potential suicide, but what I found was a convalescent who was grateful to have survived.

We went to a few cocktail parties, to dinner with a few old friends, and introduced each other to the few single men we found in our respective offices who were not nineteen. It was a restful existence, and the weeks drifted by almost without notice. Then, one afternoon, Rima rushed back early from the office, and when I came home the scent of bath oil filled the entire apartment. She had put her newest Chanel suit on the bed and was washing her emerald ring with a nail brush.

"Guess what I did today! I just felt like doing something crazy, like we used to do when we were at college, so I called Heathcliff at his office and said, 'Here I am in New York!' He had a moment of conscience—I could hear it over the phone, almost like a gulp—and then he asked me to dinner."

"Dinner? Where's his wife?"

"Evidently she's a Den Mother, whatever that is, and they have a meeting. He was going to stay and work late at the office. He says he works late at the office once or twice a week anyway, and he has to eat somewhere, so—oh, you should have heard the stammering, the excuses. He's terrified of me. Of *me*, the girl who never got anybody in her life!"

They went to an Italian restaurant where Rima had often gone with the diplomat, and where the advertising man had never been in his life. The headwaiter recognized her, with obvious respect. The menu was not only in Italian but in handwriting, and Rima took pains to explain innocently to the old Italian waiter what a certain simple dish consisted of, so that Heathcliff could stammer, "Make it two."

He missed the nine-o'clock train, and before the nine-forty-two he had bought her a white orchid. "An orchid," Rima laughed, showing it to me. "An *orchid!* I haven't had an orchid since the Senior Prom. I didn't think they made them any more."

But she put it carefully into a glass of champagne in the refrigerator, the alchemy that we had believed in our Senior Prom days would keep an orchid fresh for a week.

She had been almost silent about her affair with the diplomat, as if the gravity of first love had stunned her, but she bubbled over with her delight in Heathcliff, and I knew she had fallen in love with him before she did. "He's so square," she would say, laughing, and then add, "But he's a fox—oh, smart —watch out! I really think I'm the only one who sees the other side of him, the humor. In the advertising business they're just afraid of him, because he's so young and shrewd and on the way up. His wife's name is Dorlee—can you imagine?—and she's the same age he is, of course, because they've known each other all their lives. The old hag."

One of Rima's casual beaus, a plump young man who was also in advertising, took her to a cocktail party where Heathcliff appeared with Dorlee. "She just stood in the corner and talked to the wives," Rima told me afterward. "She looks as if she has steel fillings in her teeth. I don't think she ever shortened a dress in her life; she just wears them the way they come from the store. I heard her telling somebody that in Old Greenwich she has a TV room decorated like the inside of a ship. When she started talking about how they had to have plastic covers on everything I had to run out of the room because I nearly choked."

Heathcliff's commuting hours were irregular, for he often worked late and his two children were old enough to stay up in the TV room decorated like a ship until the captain came home to say good night. He met Rima after work several times a week. He seemed to have a calming effect on her in one way, for she stopped smoking and gave her long gold cigarette holder to our cleaning woman, who had admired it. It was a romance confined to furtive hand holding, for he was consumed by guilt and told Rima often that she was "dangerous."

"Dangerous!" she told me in delight. "Dangerous! Me, the failure, dangerous! Isn't he beautiful?"

A letter arrived from our former Washington land-lady informing Rima she was not running a storage company, and then several huge crates arrived, Railway Express collect. Rima and I stared at them with dismay. "It's either storage or my own apartment," she said, "and I think at this point, an apartment of my own might be a good idea."

She found an apartment in a new, modern building, a block from Grand Central Station. "And believe me," she said, "an apartment a block from Grand Central is not easy to find." The choice of this location was logical to her—Heathcliff could stop by for a drink every evening on his way to his train. It seems several times he had mentioned, as if he were talking about an impossible dream, that such an arrangement would be the height of bliss.

The beautiful old furniture took some of the coldness away from the boxlike rooms of this glass-and-steel monstrosity, whose only redeeming feature was that it had a working fireplace; and when I went to visit her I found the rooms once again filled with flowers. The only strange note was a small bottle with a ship inside it, which perched on the center of her spindly-legged table.

"He collects them," she said. "He gave it to me. It's kind of pretty, don't you think?"

The next time I visited Rima's apartment a block from Grand Central it was a month later. There was a man's bathrobe hanging on the hook on the bathroom door, and a can of shaving cream on the tole shelf next to the sink. A small photograph of Heathcliff stood on the table beside her bed, framed in rope.

"It's so wonderful being in love with a man near my own age," she said. "He's thirty-four, I'm twenty-six—that means when I'm seventy, he'll be only seventy-eight."

"And commuting?"

"No, of course not," she said, touching his photograph reverently. "He's never been in love before, he never cheated on her in all those years, and do you know they were both virgins when they got married? Him, too. He has a very strong sense of honor. He said he wished she would find out about us so she would do something terrible to him, because he feels he deserves it; and then he said I ought to leave him, because he deserves that; and then he said if I did leave him he might as well be dead."

"He sounds happy," I said.

"It's just his sense of honor," Rima said. "It's a man like that who makes decisions. Men *do* leave their wives, you know, but only because of great love or great guilt. And he has both. I'm glad I didn't get married last time, because I was so young I mistook romance for love. This is real love: planning a life together, being able to help someone, making someone feel alive for the first time. Before he met me, his whole life was encased in plastic, just like that horrible chintz furniture of his in the country."

Men did leave their wives, as I well knew, and

lovers left lovers, but it was neither for great love nor great guilt. Rima had been right the first time, in her letter to me: people part because of hopelessness. The death of love leads to the rebirth of another love, for love is a phoenix. A greater love does not kill a small one; it only adds pomp to the funeral.

During the following year, Rima and her advertising man tried to break up three times, but each time he came back to her, vowing he loved her more than ever and felt guiltier. She had already proposed to him several times, pretending it was only a joke, but at the end of their second year of afternoons before the train, she proposed to him seriously, and he answered her.

"How could I marry you?" he asked, tears in his eyes. "I'd bore you. You'd get tired of me. You're my elusive golden girl, and I'm just a husband and father."

"But that's what I *want*," Rima said.

"No. . . . I see you in front of the fire on a snowy night . . . I see you in that white fur coat, your eyes shining, going into the Plaza to meet an ambassador or a movie star. . . . I just don't see you in a gingham dress at the supermarket."

"Where do you think I get my food, out of flowers?"

"Yes," he answered. "And I will always bring them to you."

The transformation of Rima began that night. The next day, printed cotton slipcovers appeared on the

Louis XV chairs. She bought a huge Early American object she informed me was called an Entertainment Center, containing a 19-inch television set, a stereo phonograph with four speakers, and a radio, with a long flat surface on top that was soon covered with a collection of ships in bottles. Her Chanels and Diors were sent to a thrift shop (tax deductible) and she replaced them with tweed skirts, cashmere sweater sets, and flowered, sleeveless cotton blouses. She had pawned her emerald ring to buy the Entertainment Center, and now she wore a single strand of imitation pearls. She learned to cook tuna fish casserole with potato chips on top, and in time even a peanut butter soufflé. She saved trading stamps and redeemed them for a hobnail glass lamp with a ruffly shade, and gave her 1850 tole lamp to the cleaning woman, who ventured she'd just as soon have had the nice new one.

She washed and set her hair herself, because it was obvious Dorlee had, and she used the money thus saved to buy books called *The Sexually Satisfied Housewife* and *The Problems of the Adolescent Stepchild,* which she piled on top of the spindly-legged antique table until it broke and she replaced it with something that had formerly been a butter churn.

Her triumph came on Heathcliff's birthday. He had left his office early, and a light snow had begun to fall. At four-thirty, in the winter's early darkness, he arrived at Rima's apartment. There was snow on his coat, and he was carrying a gold-wrapped package that later turned out to contain champagne. Rima was sitting in front of the roaring fire, wearing blue jeans and toasting marshmallows.

He looked around the room as if he had never really noticed it before, still wearing his coat, still clutching the bottle of champagne in his arms. The air was fragrant with the scent of detergent and meat loaf.

"Happy birthday, honey," Rima said.

"Thank you. . . ." he murmured. "I'd better hang my coat in the bathroom; it's wet."

"Wait till you see your present! I made it."

When he came out of the bathroom he seemed more composed. He opened his present: a ship in a bottle. Rima had put the ship inside, herself. "You see," she said, "to get it in, the sails lie flat, and then I pull the string . . ."

"I know."

"Look at the marshmallow," she said. "When it's burned black like that, with the little red lights inside, it looks the way New York used to look to me at night, when I first came here—all dark and mysterious, with just those millions of little lights."

"Oh, Rima," Heathcliff whispered, holding the two bottles in his hands, the one with the ship and the one with the champagne, "I wish you had written me a poem."

She did write him a poem, the following summer, but she never gave it to him. Instead, she read it to me on the telephone. I had not seen very much of her during the winter and spring, because I had gotten a new job doing research (and my Master's degree), and she had spent most of her time in her apartment waiting for him to visit her, although the visits were fewer and farther between. We were both going to be thirty, but now it no longer seemed to matter that when Rima was thirty Heathcliff would be only thirty-eight.

"Send him the poem," I told her. "It's beautiful."

"No," she said. "I'm going to push it into one of his revolting little bottles and I'm going to toss it into the Greenwich Sound, or whatever the name is of that river he lives on. Then when he's walking in front of his split-level saying *Yo-Ho-Ho* he can find it, and see what he lost. Four years. . . . Well, last time it was five, so you can't say I'm not improving. At least it doesn't take me as long to find out I'm doomed. I am doomed, you know. I'm the girl they recite poetry to, and then in the mornings they always go back to their wives. It must be me, because I fell in love with two completely different men and neither of them wanted to stay with me."

"It's not you," I said. "Neither of them really knew what you were like. If they had, they would have loved you."

I don't know if she ever threw the bottle into the Sound, but she might have tossed it into the lake in Central Park, because all that summer Rima was addicted to long, lonely walks. Perhaps she was trying to figure things out; perhaps she was only still in her fantasy of the country wife, and the streets of the summer city were her Old Greenwich roads. I felt guilty not spending more time with her, but this time I had met someone I loved. I had not met him among the mollusks and the octogenarians; I had met him at a cocktail party. He was a producer, but he did not think lady zoologists were freaks, and I certainly did not think producers were freaks, although I had never met one before, either.

While I was occupied with the extraordinary miracle of my second (and present) love, Rima became involved in what, to her, seemed only an ordinary meeting. She had been on a long walk, it was about midnight, and she was passing Grand Central Station on her way back to her apartment when she saw a man fall down in the street. The few passers-by thought he was drunk and avoided him, but Rima went closer to see if he was ill, and discovered that he was indeed drunk. She also discovered, with delight and dismay, that he was one of her favorite authors.

"What are you doing, lying there on the curb?" she said sternly. "A great writer does not lie on the curb."

"He does if he's drunk," the author answered. He was trying to go to sleep, his cheek nestled on the sidewalk.

"You get up this minute." Rima pulled him to his feet, which was not too difficult as he was a short, wiry man, about her height, quite undernourished from too much wine, women and song. He was, she remembered reading, only four years older than she was, and she felt maternal toward him.

"Have to go to Bennington," he murmured. "Where the hell is Bennington? Have to be there in the morning."

"Bennington, Vermont?"

"Little girls' school . . . college. Lecture. Where's my train?"

"You can't lecture at Bennington like this," Rima said. She inspected his soiled clothing and bleary face with distaste. "Those girls idolize you. If they see you like this, it might ruin the rest of their lives."

"I'm . . . going to be sick."

"Good."

He decided not to be sick. "Who are you?"

"A former English major at Radcliffe, and an admirer of yours—although not at the moment. Come with me, I live around the corner." She was already leading him, his arm about her shoulders.

The writer stared at the sleeveless flowered cotton blouse, the chino walking skirt, the little strand of pearls. "Funniest-looking streetwalker I ever saw . . ." Rima slapped him.

She then took him to her apartment, a block from Grand Central, where she forced him to eat scrambled eggs and drink three cups of black coffee, and then spot-cleaned and pressed his suit while he cursed at her from a cold shower. She scanned the timetable while the writer looked around her apartment.

"You in the Waves?"

"Very funny. You can take the two-thirty train to Boston, and then there's probably a connection."

"You've even got a timetable."

"Purely for sentimental reasons," Rima said. "Here, take this aspirin and these vitamins; you'll need them later."

"You have any children?"

"No. Do you?"

"I'm not married," he said.

Suddenly, he became more than an idol or an invalid—he became a person. "You're *not?*"

"Divorced," he said.

"So am I," Rima said, "sort of."

"That's too bad. You'd make a wonderful wife. Very homey apartment. It reminds me of my mother's. You wouldn't think I had a mother, would you? Well, I do."

"You need her," Rima said. "Or a nurse. How could you possibly have gotten so drunk when you have an appointment tomorrow—or today, I should say."

"Oh!" he said, looking wildly for his jacket. "Where's the train?"

"At the station. Where are your lecture notes? Good. Your aspirin? Good. Now, take these cookies, in case you get tempted on the way."

The writer took hold firmly of Rima's arm. "You're coming with me."

"Are you crazy?"

"Yes. Come with me. I need you. I'll only be there

one day, and then we'll go to St. Thomas. I live in St. Thomas; you'll like it."

Rima looked around her apartment, the cozy, chintzy, friendly room filled with its memories of love and failure. " 'Be not afeard. The isle is full of noises, sounds and sweet airs, that give delight and hurt not.' "

"Come with Caliban," he said.

"No," Rima said, following him docilely to the door, "no, not Caliban . . . Shakespeare."

When she came back from Bennington she came to visit me, to bring me her collection of ships in bottles and to say goodbye. "When you marry that divine man you're going with, you'll have a little boy someday, and he'll like these."

"Are you really going away with him?" I asked stupidly.

"Imagine—St. Thomas! He can write his books, and I can keep house. I'll walk on the beach, and I'll send you shells if you like, if I find anything they don't have anywhere else. Imagine—he's not married —at last! He's so brilliant; I've always adored his work. I've read everything he ever wrote, and do you know what? Once, when we were in college and he had his first story published, I cut his picture out of the magazine and kept it for a year."

"Listen," I said, hating myself for it, "I read in *Time* magazine that he travels around with a Great and Good Friend. She lives in St. Thomas with him. What happened to her?"

"Oh, her!" Rima said. "He hates her. She just happens to live in St. Thomas, that's all. He says she's not a girlfriend, she's a friend girl. I saw that picture in *Time*; she looks like a squaw. She's got a braid down her back and she had this leather thong around her neck with a big tooth attached to it. I'll bet it came out of her mouth. No wonder he drank before he met me."

"He's stopped drinking?"

"One Scotch before dinner, like Heathcliff used to. Oh, I'm a reformer now." She laughed at herself, the reformer, and I wondered if life would at last be kind to her, she who could never be kind to herself.

She left the apartment, the furniture, her winter clothes, everything, and she and the writer went to St. Thomas. I went to her apartment two days before my wedding, suddenly taken by the absurdly sentimental thought that I must sell that Early American Entertainment Center and get Rima's emerald ring out of the pawn shop, if it was still there, and send it to her. I don't know why that ring seemed so important to me—perhaps because I was going to be married and I was happy, and I couldn't bear the thought of a ring Rima had worn for five years on the third finger of her left hand being misused by some stranger. But the landlord had taken possession of all the furniture in lieu of the rent she had never sent from St. Thomas, and the apartment had been sublet. Well, I thought, caught up again in my own happiness, we've both learned enough from the past, and that ring doesn't mean anything any more.

So I was married, and two years later we did have

a little boy who will like the collection of ships in bottles, when he's old enough not to break them to get the ships out. Our apartment is filled with scripts, books, records, theatrical posters, an aquarium, shells, textbooks, toys; but still there is room on the piano for Rima's collection of Battersea boxes. She had written me two happy postcards the first year, and then, nothing. I wondered if she was still in St. Thomas. Five years after she had left New York, I took a chance and wrote to her at her last address to tell her that my husband and I were going to take a winter vacation in St. Thomas, and was she still alive? She wrote back immediately.

"Yes," her letter said, "I'm still alive. Alive and single. Surprise. Look for me in the bar at your hotel any night at about ten o'clock. I'll be the one seated at the right hand of the Bard."

We arrived in St. Thomas in the afternoon. When we went down to the hotel bar that night at ten, Rima was not there. There were some pink-broiled American tourists, and a party of Italians from a large yacht that was moored in the harbor: the owner, very rich, very clean in a blue blazer, two teen-aged starlets who sat toying with the speared fruit in their drinks, two rather sinister-looking young men, and two contessas with streaks in their hair and a lot of diamonds. The Calypso trio played on a small bandstand, and the starlets got up to do whatever dance it was teen-aged starlets were doing that winter in the jet set. The contessas and their escorts looked bored because they were supposed to, and the Italian millionaire looked bored because he was. I was afraid Rima wasn't going to show up after all.

Then, at half past twelve, she arrived. She was, indeed at the right hand of the Bard, and the Bard was very, very drunk. At the left hand of the Bard, helping to support him, was a young woman the same age as Rima, with a long black braid down her back, a turtleneck T-shirt, a peasant skirt, no makeup, and a silver-and-turquoise ornament the size of a breastplate dangling from a chain around her neck. Rima had let her hair grow to her waist and braided it, her face was scrubbed and tanned, she was dressed in an almost identical village outfit, and the only difference between the two Squaw Twins was that Rima was the prettier one.

Rima let go the writer's hand and ran over to our table. Liberated, he pulled free of the other lady and went to the bar.

"Oh, I'm so glad to see you!" Rima said. "Look how pale you are—you'll have to come to the beach with me." She held her arm, the color of glistening walnut, against mine.

My husband was transfixed by the object dangling from a thong around Rima's neck. "Whose tooth is that?"

She shrugged. "I don't know. It's Olive's; we trade."

"How is everything?" I asked lamely.

"Don't ask that. I want to be happy tonight. No, it's all right, really. I'm content; I mean, I'm over him, I just stay with him because he needs me."

"Who's Olive?"

Rima glanced at her Squaw Twin. "Remember the girlfriend he said was only a friend girl? That's her. Actually, I'd go insane if I didn't have her to talk to. He's so drunk lately. And, do you know, in the beginning I really hated her? She has great individuality, though, and a crystalline intellect. She's above such things as jealousy and animosity, she really believes in the purity of non-thought. . . . oh, hell, she bores me to death."

The writer had taken the sticks away from the Calypso drummer and was crashing them on every cymbal, drum, and any surface in sight. The musicians and waiters ignored him as if he was a nightly fixture. Olive was watching him inscrutably. The Italians from the yacht looked amused.

"If I had his talent . . ." Rima said. "If I had *any* talent. . . . Tell me about New York! Tell me about the world, is it still there?"

We ordered drinks and told her about people she had known, and then we ordered more drinks and she made us tell her about people she didn't know. She was insatiable. The world, the world, what was happening outside this tiny island, this paradisiacal prison? The American tourists went up to bed, the Calypso trio disappeared, the writer and Olive were now sitting with the party of Italians from the yacht. The millionaire glanced over at us and bent toward him to whisper a question; the writer shook his head.

"How old is your baby?" Rima asked suddenly.

"Three years old."

"I'm thirty-five," Rima said. "Do I look it? Don't answer. Look—the sun's coming up, I'm going to walk on the beach."

She ran out of the bar, across the patio, across the sand, and was gone. I was afraid she might be going to drown herself and was going to run after her, but then I saw her again, wandering among the sea-grape trees, sad and alone. The writer had fallen asleep at the table, his head between the empty glasses. Olive was watching over him, totally still, a little smile at the corner of her mouth. The Italian millionaire excused himself to the group and went out to the beach.

I could see his silhouette in the pink-and-gold dawn, bowing slightly to Rima's silhouette, and then, after a moment, walking slowly beside it through the silhouettes of the sea-grape trees. The sea was all blue and gold and silver now, and in the distance the Italian's yacht rocked gently at anchor, all white.

We went up to our room. Then, suddenly, I felt one of those obsessive, extrasensory calls that are like a shout in the mind. "I'll be right back," I said, and ran down the stairs to the lobby.

The bar was closed, chairs piled on top of the tables. The Italians had all gone, and in a corner of the lobby Olive was asleep in a big chair. A yawning porter handed me a hotel envelope with my name on it, and went back behind the desk. The writer, despite his hangover, was milling around like twelve people. "Where is she? Where is she? *Rima* . . . !"

I tore open the envelope, and the tooth on the

leather thong fell into my hand. There was a note, in Rima's impeccable script: " 'When such as I cast out remorse so great a sweetness flows into the breast we must laugh and we must sing, We are blest by everything. Everything we look upon is blest.' *La donna è mobile*. Goodbye, and love."

I looked out to sea, where the yacht was only a tiny toy ship on the horizon, and then I went up to our room.

So she was gone again, with the Italian millionaire, and his starlets, and his contessas with the streaked hair. Soon, I knew, she would fall in love, and cut her braid, and toss her pueblo jewelry into the sea. She would paint her eyelids and enamel her toenails, and disappear. Once again, as always, a man who had fallen in love with a fantasy that had been created for another man would lose that fantasy, consuming it in the fire of his love. I remembered that the Rima of *Green Mansions,* for whom Rima Allen had been named, had been killed in a fire that destroyed her hiding-tree. It seemed to me, that lonely morning in St. Thomas, that the Rima I knew had been killed in many fires, rising again from the ashes of each one like a bright bird to sing the song of some wanderer's need. Had there ever been a real Rima? Born and reborn to a splendid image, she had never looked for her self, nor had anyone else. Being each man's dream of love, she had eventually failed him, and so he had failed her, and so, finally, she had failed herself.